AUTOBIOGRAPHY OF A FAMILY PHOTO

AUTOBIOGRAPHY
OF A FAMILY
PHOTO

A NOVEL

JACQUELINE WOODSON

A DUTTON BOOK

DUTTON
Published by the Penguin Group
Penguin Books USA Inc., 375 Hudson Street,
New York, New York 10014, U.S.A.
Penguin Books Ltd, 27 Wrights Lane,
London W8 5TZ, England
Penguin Books Australia Ltd, Ringwood,
Victoria, Australia
Penguin Books Canada Ltd, 10 Alcorn Avenue,
Toronto, Ontario, Canada M4V 3B2
Penguin Books (N.Z.) Ltd, 182–190 Wairau Road,
Auckland 10, New Zealand

Penguin Books Ltd, Registered Offices:
Harmondsworth, Middlesex, England

First published by Dutton, an imprint of Dutton Signet,
a division of Penguin Books USA Inc.
Distributed in Canada by McClelland & Stewart Inc.

First Printing, January, 1995
10 9 8 7 6 5 4 3 2 1

Poem reprinted with permission
of Simon & Schuster from For
Colored Girls Who Have Considered
Suicide/When the Rainbow Is Enuf
by Ntozake Shange. © 1975, 1976,
1977 by Ntozake Shange.

Portions of this novel were awarded the Kenyon Review Award for Literary Excellence in
Fiction and have previously appeared in The Kenyon Review, The American Voice and
American Identities: A Bread Loaf Anthology.

 REGISTERED TRADEMARK—MARCA REGISTRADA

LIBRARY OF CONGRESS CATALOGING-IN-PUBLICATION DATA
Woodson, Jacqueline.
    Autobiography of a family photo / Jacqueline Woodson.
        p.   cm.
    ISBN 0-525-93721-8
    1. Afro-American families—New York (N.Y.)—Fiction.   2. Family
violence—New York (N.Y.)—Fiction.   3. Brooklyn (New York, N.Y.)—
Fiction.   4. Girls—New York (N.Y.)—Fiction.   I. Title.
PS3573.O64524A94   1995
813'.54—dc20   94-3639
                                                                    CIP

Printed in the United States of America
Set in Sabon
Designed by Leonard Telesca

PUBLISHER'S NOTE

Acknowledgments

Always, I thank those who helped me through the early stages of this, including Teresa Calabrese, Alpha Kappa Alpha Sorority, Carole DeSanti, Charlotte Sheedy, Linda Villarosa, Sarah Schulman, Cathy Mckinley, Jennie Livingston, Alicia Henry, Michelle Adams, Tim Seibles, Sarah Gray Thompson, and The MacDowell Colony.

'Dark phrases of womanhood
of never havin been a girl
half-notes scattered
without rhythm/no tune
distraught laughter fallin
over a black girl's shoulder
it's funny/it's hysterical
the melody-less-ness of her dance

—Ntozake Shange

AUTOBIOGRAPHY
OF A FAMILY
PHOTO

The Daily News

I died once. And then I died again. And then, death had no hold on me.

Simple.

As simple as this: Yesterday I woke up and the sky was full of blues, changing, arching over themselves. Sitting there, I watched it. And this is what I was thinking: This girl sitting here with her arms wrapped around her legs is not a girl but a woman. And in the woman there are a million girls bottled, muted. A million half-lives, some skirted but bare-chested, others naked. Some with dark arms reaching upward, others stooped into bending, still as glass. A million girls. Dark. Bellowing. Multiplying. Chaos. Hari-kari. War.

It's inevitable.

And this sky is not a sky but simply the color blue, the chaos of blue, the inevitability of blue—sky, lake, mallard, sea.

Sea. Simple as . . .

My first death was a slow one. I read about it in the *Daily News*.

Here is the story:

I was in love with a boy. Franklin Thomas. Simple. In fifth grade love is simple—a shared piece of food at lunch, someone calling your name across the school yard, the first warm day of spring, coats draping from heads, a jump-rope game in which you make sure to falter on the first letter of the name of your sweetheart. AB—CD—EF . . . Then you and Franklin are sitting in a tree *k-i-s-s-i-n-g*. Even if you're growing up in a city where trees are so thin-limbed, the thought of you and the person you love sitting in one is unimaginable.

But you imagine it anyway.

Mallard. . . .

In fifth grade, Franklin was perfect. His father, a teacher, had married Sandra's mother. Sandra was also in our class and this seemed to make everything so much more perfect.

"You guys eat together?" we would ask Sandra and Franklin at recess, our eyes bright and pleading. *If this could only be us.* And Franklin and Sandra would smile, nod, look at us, and away. At us. And away.

Down the hall, Franklin's brother was in a second grade classroom with Sandra's sister. Sometimes their parents dropped them off and though we had never in all of our ten years imagined it could happen like this, there it was—a white man smiling into the eyes of his beautiful black wife. Slowly, our minds wrapped around this and we huddled in groups of three and four in the corners of classrooms and school yards to imagine such a thing.

Lake. . . .

When you die young, your life doesn't end. It becomes a different thing. Another layer is added by the process of taking away.

Sandra's beautiful, beautiful mother was found . . .

Someone brought the *Daily News* to school and even those of us still caught up in the beauty of it all, struggled through the tight knots of fifth graders to get a look at the words printed there. A tiny article, black letters on white paper. Simple.

The night before I bought a silver-plated necklace. A silhouette of a boy and a girl in profile, their lips outstretched in a kiss, and had engraved upon it my name and Franklin's. Maybe he would lift the necklace over his head, press the charm underneath his shirt, against his heart. . . . *Yes*, I thought, *it could happen like this*. Love for a dollar—an extra fifty cents for the engraving, the jeweler pulling my ribboned braid and asking with a smirk, "Is Franklin your boyfriend?" And me answering softly, "Maybe. I don't know."

Death is the thing that pulls back the skin of another life making visible the blood of it. And bone.

Sandra and Franklin were absent. Maybe the rumors were true. And now, the *Daily News* telling the story we had heard whispered all morning. A graham cracker going dry behind my teeth. Milk with a paper straw warming at my desk.

"Let me have a look," someone is whispering. And in the hall, our teacher surrounded by other teachers, their voices hushed and solemn. In my desk, a tiny white box and inside that box, a chain from a different time, another life before the skin was scraped back exposing everything beneath it . . . to air.

Sandra's mother was found in bed with her daughters. Three bullets in her chest, her daughters moaning softly, clutching her still body. Cold. Blue-black with death. Sea-black. Black as lake water.

Franklin's father had been arrested. Manslaughter. A jealous rage.

"Let me see," someone is insisting. And now, turning away from the article, I let another someone push past me. Outside, the sky is the color of steel, heavy and hard.

I died once when I was ten and in the death words tossed themselves at me, blurring in their wake.

Sky. Became the term for blue. Perfection, a synonym for rage. Simplicity, the bark-colored darkness behind closed eyes.

And then I died again. But this was a different death— hushed. Billowing. Vague. Its silence shook me open. What tumbled from me was this: The snapshots of who I was, and a million little girls, already old and full of the hollow places growing takes us to.

This world can hold a million girls in its hand.

This world can drop them.

The White House

My mother cradles a pale newborn baby swaddled in blue and tells the others that this is the newest addition to our family. My big sister, Angel, begs to hold him so my mother makes her sit down on the edge of the sofa before placing the tight bundle in her lap. Still, Angel drops our baby brother and he lands with a thump on the carpeted floor. Nobody shouts but my mother's dark face ashes over as we wait for the tinny baby scream that finally breaks into the silence. Our mother rocks him, presses kisses across his yellow-brown forehead. Maybe, she too is crying.

After that we are not allowed to touch our baby brother. *Not even to kiss him*, our mother says. But the four of us, Angel, Carlos, Troy and me, watch this baby. And wait.

There is something different about this one, seven-year-old Angel says.

Yes, Carlos, who is a year older, agrees, pressing his heavy, dark-brown hand against the baby's pale throat. *Something very different.*

Troy, the oldest brother, is almost sixteen. He is the beautiful one, graceful and thin as ribbon. Old men watch him and lick their lips. Mama says, *I don't know where I went wrong with that one* and loves him up. Beautiful, beautiful Troy. Can you marry your brother? He says I'm the only girl he'll ever love. "I don't care about that baby," he whispers, leaning into the crib to get a better look. "No half-white nothing's gonna do much for me. And look how easily white bruises." He pinches the baby hard until the skin on his neck turns bright red. When the baby cries out, we run off, out of Mama's reach.

"If you're white," Troy whispers late at night, when it is only us awake in the darkness. "You can be President. That's the only thing different."

So at three, I am waiting. Maybe the pale, pale baby will grow up to be President. And move us all into the White House.

Dreams

APRIL 1, 1967

There is a house on our block. A brown and gold house with graffiti on the front door and a broken-down fence squeaking on rusted hinges.

You ever wonder where dreams go to die?

Late at night, I lie in bed wondering about that house, about the family that lived there once and where their dreams went. Angel rolls over and whispers, "Go to sleep and stop mumbling in the night like you're crazy."

In the morning when I ask her about dreams she closes her eyes and pretends she is still sleeping. And Troy? He says when you get to be a certain age, *boom!* Dreaming just stops. *I used to dream all over the place, girl. And look at me.* He looks down at himself, picking at the foam sprouting from the torn-up couch in the living room. *I ain't nothing.* He says it like it's the most obvious thing in the world and I should know this.

But I don't.

Every night I think about that house and wonder if the family that lived there once ever had dreams, big dreams. Dreams of driving fine cars back into this neighborhood so they can say, "Hey, look what we've gone and did!" And every day I sit on the front stoop and watch and wait.

Maybe a red Mercedes will cruise on by.

The War

Troy is the oldest one. For his eighteenth birthday he gets a letter. My father reads it slowly. Behind him, my mother is moaning. Rocking and moaning and cursing God.

"The war will make a man out of you," he says.

We watch Troy from the second-floor window, all of us piled against each other, until he and my father are out of sight.

"If he didn't go," Carlos says, "he would have been a faggot."

"Yeah," Angel agrees, her hand on my shoulder. "No faggots in the family."

At night, Troy waits until my mother and father are asleep before he sneaks a pair of heels from my mother's closet and prances around our room in them.

"When I come back from over there," Troy whispers, winking, "I'm gonna do myself up right. Makeup. Some fly clothes. Be stepping *out*!"

Angel and I lie on our high-riser pretending to be asleep until we both start giggling so loud, we have to cover our heads with our pillows. Across the room, Carlos sits up on his top bunk and stares at Troy fascinated. "Boys don't wear heels," he whispers.

"This boy does," Troy whispers back. "This faggot fairy punk and whatever else people call me behind my back— well, I got news for them. This Vietnam boy steps out in *leather* pumps, not those half-rubber shits." He lifts his foot to admire Mama's shoe. "Vietnam can kiss my ass."

He says the word softly. *Vietnam.* And it makes me think of the short pink sausages that Mama treats us to sometimes. The ones we eat right out of the can, mushing them onto saltines. It makes me think of that Sunday night with the television turned down low and all five of us on the carpeted living-room floor with three cans of those sausages watching *The Children's Hour* all the way up till the end when the woman hangs herself. Then Mama made us turn the television off and Angel said she'd never eat those sausages again because after that movie, they tasted awful to her. But me and Carlos and Troy still eat them even though after that, they always make me think of women in attics, swinging slowly, back and forth.

"Bring me back some sausages, Troy," I say. And Angel looks at me.

"I'd bring you anything you wanted, girl," Troy says. "From anywhere. When I come back from over there, we're gonna party."

Cory gurgles in his sleep until Angel goes over to his crib and brings him back to bed with her.

Don't let the baby see him, Carlos warns. Angel covers his closed eyes with her hand.

———

When I come back from over there. But you didn't know, did you, Troy, that no one would come back whole? Cruising all those beautiful, beautiful black boys surrounding you. Left. Left. Left Right Left. My back is aching. My belt's too tight. My booty's shaking from left to right. Gook's nest. Gook's head. Scalp. Scalp. Hey, Troy, let's go out and get some pussy tonight. Nah, man, I'm gonna stay here and write home. What are you, a faggot? These women hotter than July and you talking 'bout writing home. Beautiful, beautiful bodies surround me, you wrote. This is what hell must be like—something you wanting right there in your reach but you better not touch it. And the smell of skin on fire. Hey, girl, my skin's on fire. . . .

Troy takes a suit from the closet in our bedroom and makes me put it on over my pajamas. "Oh, girl, you would be a beautiful boy," he says, standing behind me in the mirror. "All you need is a tie." In the near-darkness, I am afraid of the image I see. *I could be a boy*, I am thinking. *It's as easy as that.* Then Troy makes me dance with him, silently and stiffly around the bedroom until the others are laughing.

A month later, Troy disappears into the dawn of some silvery morning and waves to us from the back of a bus loaded down with somber men.

"Good riddance to the queen," Carlos says. But he stays in bed until late in the afternoon, and we walk careful around him, trying hard to ignore the gulping sound he makes when he cries.

Accidents

C arlos assures me I wasn't an accident. He says I was a
plan, a sneaky-woman plan my mother devised to get
my father to stay. "Daddy said that's how women are. They
plan stuff behind your back."

Carlos peers into the mirror above our dresser. "My eyes
are baby blue," he says. "Wonder how I got baby blue eyes."

My father's eyes are brown and soft as the Sonny Rollins
records he plays, sitting upstairs in the living room, drumming his fingers against his knees—his dark face flat and
calm. When he looks at me and Angel, there is fear behind
his gaze. Maybe he thinks we will hurt him somehow. I want
to run to where he is and promise him that we won't. I want
to scream, *Nobody's gonna plan stuff, Daddy.* But even as
Carlos and I talk, my father is leaving, cruising in his cab
down some faraway street. *Can we go, today, Daddy? It's
Saturday. Please? Please?*

*You all need to stay home. It's too cold. It's too hot. It's
too damp or dry. . . . C'mon, Carlos. You're strong enough*

to ride with your old man. Grinning. The man-to-man grin for Carlos. Carlos—his first real son since Troy is—as he and Mama whisper—gonna be "that way." Look at me, Daddy. Without the fear. What's there to be scared of? Two boys. Two girls. Perfect for a while. Then Troy turning different and Cory born half-white. Where did he go wrong? How could he have a family like this and still feel like a man? Those soft brown eyes melting into silence and a saxophone holding a note like someone screaming until his fingers stop drumming and he drifts up into the note and vanishes. . . .

The years take off. Fly.

A woman knocks on the apartment door of a building smelling of vomit. An apartment door nestled in the corner of a neighborhood that was born a ghetto, ambushed by poverty and left to rot. The broken neighbors peeping out from battered windows, silent as death.

Now the soft shoe of an old man walking on linoleum and now, the door creaking open and the woman's nose filling with the smell of cigarette smoke.

"Daddy?"

And the man staring from behind the crack in the door, gray, withered, suspicious.

"Daddy, it's me . . ."

Strangers embrace, talk softly and guarded.

"I had to stop driving that cab when my legs gave out. Look, you've gone and cut off all your hair but you still look good. How's your mama?"

"She lost her voice."

"She should gargle . . ."

"No, she doesn't speak at all. Been that way for almost eight years. . . ." Words like music, taking off, thin, dead as gauze.

"I see Carlos every once in a while. But you and your sister . . . and Cory but he don't really . . . no, he wasn't mine. Heard he got a good job though. . . ."

In the distance, a truck horn. Beyond that, silence.

I tell Carlos his eyes are brown, dark brown like everyone else in the family. I tell him I don't care about accidents, don't care about anything. I say this while I twirl a piece of string uncertainly between my stumbling six-year-old fingers. I say this as if I really don't care.

The house is empty, tight and empty as the inside of somebody's shoe.

Carlos squints into the mirror then opens his eyes wide. "Baby blue. Dark, dark blue. Sometimes that color looks brown, you know. It's hard to tell." He turns away from the mirror and gives me a long look. I am sitting on the edge of Troy's bed—a bunk bed. The top belongs to Carlos. The top bunk sags. Carlos is chubby, dark brown. He and Angel have the same hair—more curly than nappy, soft blue-black hair that shines without oil. Troy and I have our mother's kinky hair, our father's slitted eyes.

"Mama wanted him to stay. Daddy told me. Man-to-man. Says Mama figured if she had one more kid, that would do it. So he stayed. Least for now. But he'll be gone soon."

"I don't care." My voice wavers.

Carlos touches my shoulder. His hand slips down, grazes my chest, pauses. Last summer my mother made a mistake and bought him a T-shirt with a man's face on it. Only the man's eyes were breasts. Angel noticed this. "Those eyes are titties," she said, pointing. Carlos looked down at his shirt. He stared at the breasts for a long time until my mother made him take the shirt off. The breasts were pale with pinkish nipples. "It was on sale," my mother said. "Maybe that's why it was so cheap."

Carlos's hand slips over and comes to rest at the place where a breast would be if I had any. I can hear his breath, coming fast. Heavy ten-year-old breath hovering above my fear. Otherwise, there is silence. Emptiness and silence. "Titties are cheap," he says. "You can get them on sale."

Maybe he is lying.

The Things He Turns to Gold

JANUARY 8, 1970

M y little brother Cory slams into our bedroom in the middle of "The Brady Bunch" to announce that he wants to be a helicopter when he grows up. My other siblings are only half listening but I give him my full attention even though any word spoken in the next half hour could decrease Jan Brady's chances of becoming a Fillmore Junior High School cheerleader.

"We could be like the Bradys," Angel says dreamily, moving the dark mass of straightened hair covering her shoulders away from her face. Jan is wearing a ponytail. Angel pulls her own hair back, gazes at the television, then sighs. "We only need one more kid in our family."

Carlos's eyes follow Jan's every move. He is silent, transfixed. At ten, he is the oldest now that Troy is gone. Carlos tells us he is working on a plan—a *maybe* that will make us like the Brady Bunch, radiant and ranch-housed in a quiet suburb bubbling over with baking maids and station wagons.

"All I need is a propeller," Cory says. My sister whirls

around, throwing a finger to her lips, and his voice drops as he kneels beside me in the blue TV light to tell me his scheme.

"I would fly," he says. "All over everything and everybody. High like a kite, only higher."

The small difference in our years defines us, makes us allies.

"No black boy ever grew up to be a helicopter!" I say, but my little brother's small face locks into a stubbornness not allowed in the presence of our parents, a stubbornness the four of us reserve for each other.

"I *want* to be one. It's like a super hero only you're a helicopter. You fly around and you save people's *lives*." He is still whispering but Angel glares at us, and his voice drops even lower. "You have a radio-mouth that goes 'Danger— Danger Everywhere!' "

On the television, Jan's big brother Greg coaches her through a cheer, screaming, "Louder Jan, Louder!"

Cory moves to the far end of our bedroom and sinks down against the wall. I follow him, sink down beside him. "Anyway, I'm only half-black."

His face flickers bright, darkens, flickers bright, darkens —brown-gold with hair curling a darker brown around his ears.

I know this—that a part of him is white, a part we know nothing about. A part my mother and father argue about in the early morning. Suspecting us asleep, their voices waft past the thin walls like smoke, settling above our beds in violent whispers. And we learn Cory is our mama's lie showing up white as spilled salt then fading into a pale, pale amber. *Still the traces*, my father says. Still the proof that a black man can't leave his woman for one minute without her making a fool out of him.

We are hungry for the other half of him, the secret of him, the essence of his whiteness. But settle for staring. We stare at this brother when we think he isn't looking, drinking in his whiteness like milk; the soft bark-colored curl of his hair, the flecks of gold in his eyes and beneath the thin layers of his skin. We think, maybe this is the part of our lineage that connects us with the Bradys. The part that makes us unusual, thus somehow better than white-deficient families. This part that disconnects us from our own dark selves with a promise of something paler.

"The other half of me," Cory says, "is different."

I move closer to him, press my nose against his neck. He smells of baby oil and sweat. For the moment, the four of us are silent. I would like to peel the amber skin away and drink in the gold beneath it.

"You could be a statue," I say. "People would spend all of their time looking at you." And Cory freezes in his position and smiles.

"Yeah," he says. "A statue."

Angel flings her hair away from her face, Marsha Brady-style, then drops her head so that again, it falls across her eyes. "No you can't," she says. "You're different but not different enough," she says.

Cory leans against my shoulder to cry. Maybe he realizes he's stuck with us, right here on the ground.

On the television, Brady Bunch music begins to play. My big brother puts both of his thumbs in his mouth and begins to rock as the credits start to roll.

This House

APRIL 23, 1971

Keep walking. Past the gap in the front fence where a gate used to whine in the summer heat until, rusted and dangerous, its coiling iron bars let go of themselves and fell, landing heavily on my baby brother's left foot. Even now, he limps through this life although he won't let himself remember the accident, the whys and hows of it. But knows it had something to do with me swinging on the gate, falling with it, the howls of my mother curling from the upstairs window, until Cory, screaming and pale, collapsed too. Now Angel calls that "the summer of collapses." My baby brother limps, has part of a toe missing on his left foot and remembers what he wants to when he wants to. Sometimes he doesn't remember anything and those are the good days, Angel tells me.

Slowly.

Keep walking.

Now you're inside. Our house. Straight through downstairs, each room dropping off into the next one. Narrow walls painted pale shades of blue, beige and green. Through to the back stairs. Up there, the rooms just miss each other, separated by tiny hallways. The bathroom and the kitchen falling off like links.

But down here is different. Down here there are no tiny hallways. Down here, each room bumps right into the next. No doors. Windows, with silver bars and ragged shades and off-colored curtains billowing thin, pathless as smoke.

Sometimes when there is no one here, upstairs or down, I scream until the back of my throat swells over. Once my little brother limped in, his arms overloaded with the stuffed animals he has collected in his five years of living. *Hey*, he said, *what the hell is wrong with you?*

Nothing. I said. *I thought I was alone.*

This City

Upstairs, Mama is playing an Al Green record over and over and over until the music seeps into the walls. I hear her feet shuffling and imagine her doing a slow dance with the broom, her distant gaze looking out past the bay windows. Maybe this isn't what she dreamed when she packed her two gray vinyl suitcases and got on a bus heading North.

Mama holds fast to the soft pull of the South. Dragging her Yeses down into *will you please*, her high cheeks rising, scraping against a brightness in her eyes—the way a knife plunging over and over into a dull surface relinquishes its sharpness. But when she laughs, I think, *this is how I want to learn to laugh—forcing laughter up and out of me*. Like a moan. Like a prayer.

Now her light blue housedress is torn at the shoulder. When she can't find a scarf, she puts a pair of panties on her head and we all pray silently that she doesn't make a mistake and go outside wearing them. Maybe no other mother in this city wears panties on their head—the white cotton briefs with ragged elastic leg holes.

Lay your head upon my pillow. Al Green is singing and Mama is moving softly, remembering the sweet green oaks that grew down South in Grandma's front yard. She whispers *I don't want to die here* and forgets that a long time ago when she was just a girl, she thought if she didn't make it to the big city, she'd absolutely die.

All of her old friends are up in Harlem but she was afraid of the dangerous joy that end of the world promised her so she settled for Brooklyn, a quiet block of two-family houses, back porches, an urban piece of the past nestled in cement.

When I am alone with her she tells me she believes in dreams, that everybody has them and her biggest one is to own a house somewhere, maybe Hollis, Queens, or Laurelton, where the rats don't dance between the floorboards at night. Last Sunday, we went with her and Daddy—the whole family piled onto the train, then a bus for a half hour to a real estate office. But the white man who had promised them something better over the phone glared at us, said he didn't have a key to the place. Daddy listened, nodding, his Adam's apple bobbing up and down. I wish I knew the really big words—like for the quiet that's thick enough to touch or that thing that happens to Daddy's face when he's around white people. I wish I knew how Al Green gets away with hitting those high notes and nobody says, "Man, what a faggot." While that man talked, we stood, all of us holding hands across the office floor like Red Rover Red Rover, waiting for the other team to send somebody over. And if we had really been playing that game, and it was that real estate man they sent over? I would have made a fist out of me and Angel's hand, held on so tight, he would have been sorry he ever thought about breaking through. But we stood there,

Mama, Carlos, Cory, me, Angel and Daddy, like guards, squeezing each others' hand, silent as death.

But after that, Mama's eyes closed over, just snapped off like a light.

Now, upstairs alone with Al Green, she is imagining new colors for the gray-green walls and my father is off driving a cab. He's gonna get a job at the post office soon and that's a good job, everybody says. Daddy tells us he has a friend who works at the post office who just bought a house in Far Rockaway.

This city is bright orange today, summery and loud.

"Don't go upstairs," Angel says, coming into the kitchen where I am sitting staring at a glass half-filled with soda. "Mama's in one of her moods."

Al Green creeps down the peeling plaster and settles at the table with me. Mama bought the record a week ago. She hasn't stopped playing it since.

David

My big brother tells me that David is a white boy with black boy's hair. On a cool autumn morning, I am standing in front of my building, watching David sweep red, gold and brown leaves into the gutter. His Afro blows with the first warm gust of wind and I shiver, feeling my stomach churn, hoping David turns, looks at me. Please, David, look at me. I've combed my hair into two cornrows that circle my head. Silver moons dangle from my ears. Bright blue elephant bell-bottoms that my friend Marianna swears give me a nice ass. Gray leatherlike platform shoes. A blouse tight enough to hug my chest, dark enough to hide the tissue paper replacing nonexistent breasts.

David sweeps slowly. Inside, my mother tells me he sweeps this way because his brain is dead on one side of his head. "Don't talk to him," my mother says. "Don't even go near him." I nod when she says this, then race outside again, a peach ripe as summer in my hand.

Over and over again, David sweeps one spot, like Sisyphus, the leaves circling back around him, landing at his feet. I take a bite and watch him. A white black boy. Blond Afro. Blue eyes. Thin pale lips. No ass.

The block is silent, warm. The air blowing around me smells of summer.

"My mama says don't talk to you," I yell when David moves with his broom closer to my gate.

David looks at me, pale, so pale . . . bits of blond hair spiraling from beneath his nose, his white boy lips curling into a smile.

"Hey, sweet girl. What's your name? Go ask your mama if she wants me to sweep." His voice, deep and gravelly as a black man's.

I take a step back, focus on the sidewalk. Little Sally Walker Sitting on a Saucer. Rise Sally Rise. Wipe Your Weepy Eyes. Turn to the East. Turn to the West. Turn to the Boy That You Like the Best.

"Will you be my lover in ten years, sweet girl?" When I look up, David is winking, a grin full of white teeth and dimples.

David sweeps past me, slides sloe blue eyes in my direction and grins again, singing "Why Can't We Be Friends?" Behind me, like a hot breath, I feel Mama's gaze on my back, watching, guarding her baby girl against crazy men. But her gaze can't hold back the years, can't rip desire away, can't hold on . . .

Maybe she knows that soon the tight beginnings of breasts will replace the tissue and the longing will callous over into a need no fantasy can appease.

Fifteen. Head pressed against the pane of Mama's living-room window. Waiting. The house empty, full of Parliament blasting away "We want the funk/Gotta have some funk."

David rounding the corner, broom in hand as though seven years haven't slipped past. Raising the window, calling his name. "What are you, David? Conceited? Can't say hello?" In the way I've learned to flirt from other teenagers. Then more coyly, a whisper, calling down: "You want to come hear some P-Funk?", already twisting my hair out of the silly young girl braids. Expectant. Ready.

David's voice moving over the music, "You sure your mother ain't around?" a pale calloused hand pushing the hair away from my eyes, so close I smell his breath, wild cherry Lifesaver sweet, thin lips moving toward me, "I could get arrested, girl," but still his hand underneath my shirt, groping for the tiny, tiny breasts that have just begun to round out into something.

"How old you say you was anyway, sweet girl?"

"Old enough to be lying here."

My mother's bed soft beneath us, David's armpits, sweet musk as though he'd never touched deodorant, arms lifting up, moving over me, "Open your legs, baby." My legs inching apart, his fingers deep in the sparse hair, pressing into a place so painful I cry out.

"You're ready. You're almost ready." Then his fingers in my mouth tasting of me, smelling of me and me gagging in disgust, choking back the pain, getting it mixed up with the pleasure of the weight of him.

"You're ready, sweet girl." Taking my tongue between his fingers like a straw. Sucking it, drawing me deeper into him. Pressing into me thick and hard. The smell of Lifesavers long gone, replaced now by something acrid, dense, heated. So much heat and weight and searing pleasure.

"David, this hurts."

Slow motion, in and out of me with such a desperation, willing me to hold on with a strength that is new and foreign as this moment, my arms circling his back, legs spread, face

buried between his neck and shoulder, inhaling, exhaling.
David's tongue warm along my shoulder. "Don't stop, Da-
vid." In the background, Bootsy Collins leading P-Funk into
jam after jam after jam.

"Sweet, sweet girl."

"Will you?" David asks again, resting his chin on the tip
of his broom.

"Yes," I whisper, already at eight feeling desire, like a
trash can fire, blowing a hot breeze in my direction. "But my
mama says I can't talk to you . . . now."

Where My Mother Touches Me

DECEMBER 25, 1971

Christmas Day I pull the bow from my first present. My mother's camera flashes on me cross-legged in a flannel bathrobe underneath the tree. The robe belongs to my father and even as she flashes, I can hear my mother suck her teeth at the fact that I can't keep my eight-year-old body out of my father's clothes. I hold the box up and smile. Then shake it, knowing already there will be a doll inside, probably one that eats and pees with the unformed body of an infant and the blond, straight hair of an offspring that could never, even by the minutest possibilities, have been brought into this world by someone as dark and kinky-haired as myself.

Carlos pulls a Lionel train set from underneath the tree. I quickly drop my box and scurry to help him put it together.

"Open your own presents," my mother says. But there is a weariness behind the command that is becoming more familiar to me.

"I know it's a *doll*."

"What else would it be?" Then my mother and father are

arguing about creative thought in gift giving but their voices drift off. Angel opens the box for me and pulls a brown-skinned baby doll from plastic wrapping.

Distracted for a moment, I snatch it back from her.

The doll's hair is jet black, cascading down her back like hair I've never seen on a black person. I run my fingers through it. Yellow-brown tiger eyes stare blankly up at me. I cradle the doll in my arms and my mother's camera flashes on this. In the weeks to follow, the doll will be added to my collection of useless toys, assembled to dust on the shelf above my bed. When I am thirteen I will be punished for disassembling every doll I own and reassembling them so that black dolls have white arms, white dolls have black legs and none of them have clothes or hair. I will run the dolls over with my brother's trains, hold them over the stove until their plastic skin melts away from itself, dripping into a smelly sizzle over the open flame. *Hey girl, my skin's on fire.* Then I will pack all of the dolls up in an old pillowcase and put them out in the trash.

But for now, I rock the doll stiffly, pull a smile across my face, hold it until my mother's camera flashes, hold it while circles flicker and burn bright red before my eyes.

"That'll be a nice picture," my mother says.

But long after my mother's flash, I am still standing with the doll, incarcerated into this posture, afraid to move a step in any direction out of her frame. Afraid all of a sudden, to blur this image of me.

Getting Stoned

"What's 'getting stoned'?" I ask.

We are sitting in a circle in our bedroom with my sister Angel in the center rolling pot she has just bought from the boy who paces the abandoned lot at the corner of our block whispering "Sess! Sess! I got your Sess! Joints and nickel bags." The boy has the greasy black hands of a mechanic that contrast strangely with the thin white sticks of pot and squares of yellow bags he produces for the approval of passersby.

Angel cocks an eyebrow. "It's when people throw rocks at you." Then she and Carlos exchange looks and laugh.

Carlos stares wide-eyed as she expertly twists the pot into tissue paper, licks it and holds it up in front of her face to admire.

"Where'd you learn how to do that?" he asks.

"From wherever."

"Is it dope?" This is my baby brother asking, his soft brown eyes wide with fear.

Angel glares at him. "No, it's not dope, stupid, but you still can't have any. And if you breathe one word to anybody, I'll kick your ass around the block and back again."

My baby brother's face folds into something between anger and humiliation—a frown maybe, or the beginning of a hard cry. "I'ma tell Mama you cursed."

"Shut up," Carlos and Angel say at the same time.

I take my baby brother's hand in my own. "I don't want any either," I whisper.

"You're such a coward," my sister says, lighting the joint and sucking the smoke deep into her chest. She squints when she does this. After a moment, she passes the joint to my big brother and exhales. "Just suck on it and hold it."

"Just suck on it and hold," I mock.

They ignore me, passing the joint back and forth until the room is filled with a yellow haze of sweet-smelling smoke and the joint is no more than a spot of paper burning the tip of my big sister's fingers.

"Now what happens?" I ask.

My big sister and brother exchange looks and start laughing as though they are being tickled.

"Look at her ears," my big sister coughs between peals of laughter.

"Look at *his*!"

My little brother puts his head down, covers his ears with his hands.

"They are so stupid-looking."

The laughter grows louder. Then my sister is coughing and tearing. "They're so weird. I need water."

She stumbles to the kitchen, returns with a tall glass of water and a bag of popcorn.

"You want some?"

My big brother nods, takes the bag from her and tilts it up, pouring popcorn into his mouth.

"I want some," I say, holding out my cupped hands.

They look at me, my sister's eyes bright. She takes a kernel from the bag and hands it to me. This sends them both into another fit of laughter.

I roll my eyes, look away as though I could care less about being in the same room with them. My little brother is crying.

"I'm telling," he says, sniffing back snot.

"Don't be a crybaby," I whisper. "It's not anything."

But the distance in their eyes scares me. There is an apathy behind it I don't yet understand.

My sister leans back on her elbows and looks at us as though taking us in from a distance.

"You both . . ." she begins. "You two . . ."

Then she is laughing again and my big brother is laughing with her. "I don't even know what I was gonna say!"

"You both . . . are so stupid," my big brother laughs. "How could we even be related?"

"What if somebody comes home?" I say, scared of their hysteria, groping for the sanity a parent provides but afraid still to be caught, knowing that my presence here is in itself incriminating.

Nineteen. Home from school for the summer. My mother is silent and the doctors can't tell us why. My father has slipped off. And each of us has taken what we've wanted from this bedroom and moved on. Sitting here alone, against this wall, folding pot into tissue for my own private consumption, I stop suddenly, mid-roll, and remember that day was the beginning of an absence of grown-ups, a beginning of the four of us alone because our parents had begun to hate each other—had begun to hate the spaces in their lives that children could not fill.

"Nobody's coming," my sister mumbles. Behind her eyes there is so much distance that I want to ask her *What happened to your other eyes?*

She glares at me and says, "It's like everybody just ran away."

Carlos

There is a word for the way we pull the world apart. Angel spells it in a spelling bee and gets first prize. Deconstruct. *D-e-c-o-n.* . . .

But at eight, I don't understand yet, how it works. How the simple things can become more complicated until even someone as smart as Angel can't get ahold of something.

"Pull the world apart," Angel says, showing off. "Syllable by syllable, phrase by phrase, word by word. Break it down."

Sitting in the bathtub, counting the stages of my growing, three new pubic hairs, a soreness behind my nipples that may mean the beginning of breasts, I pull my body apart, phase by phase, thinking *This is mine. This all belongs to me.*

Precarious. The door that shelters me in this privacy is held on by rusted hinges and a latch carelessly drilled into a rotting wall. This privacy, this growing, this shelter behind the door beneath the water can so suddenly be destroyed. This is what it means to be eight and naked, perched in a small space. All of this happening in the tiny room that is only a sink, a claw-foot tub, and the blue-white porcelain toilet.

"Toilet," I whisper.

From the other side of the door, my big brother calls my name, softly at first, then louder and louder. I splash my washcloth into the bathwater, squeeze it against my chest, let the lukewarm water drip down.

"Let me in," my brother says softly, although no one else is home. "I have to go."

"I'm almost finished," I call through the door. Then whisper again, "toilet."

"I have to go now, please. I want to show you something."

"No."

"Please . . ."

"No."

Then there is quiet. Almost quiet, except for the word. "Toilet" beating out its own rhythm against the back of my throat. "To-i-let."

If I change it, the first *T* to a *D*, then the word would be different, would take over itself, this moment, me.

My brother is back again. My stomach moves beneath the washcloth.

"Go away. Let me take a bath."

"I have to go."

I hear the sound of scraping, see the beginning of the flat silver blade of the knife moving underneath the latch, then up, until it is flipping the latch from its eye and the door is opening and my big brother is slipping inside the bathroom, relatching it, turning, his thing hanging from his zipper, dark, wrinkled, still.

Do-I-let.

"Get out of here, I'm taking a bath."

"Stop being stupid. Just let me do the thing and I'll let you finish being by yourself. You been in here too long anyway."

Then I am standing, a million miles away but there, above the still, half-cold bathwater, my legs spread, shoulders, arms, hands dripping waiting for him to finish rubbing his thing between the space there. Waiting, waiting, dripping, staring off.

There are places you can go to when it happens to you.

At the park, in the classroom, in front of candy stores, we gather in groups of soft-speaking girls.

"Something happens to me . . . when I am alone with . . ."

"So what?" someone says. "Like it don't happen to everybody?"

Kicking heels against ground to swing out and up over everything, another says, "Let's make believe we can fly."

And I kick off too, feeling the wind take me, brushing like feathery hands against my face, arms, eyelashes, hair.

"Sometimes . . ."

When I try to tell them about it, my friends don't let me say who it is. They say there are places you can go to and in a sense it's the same as saying it happens to everybody, including boys, that no one's immune.

My friends circle me, touch my shoulders, my hair, run their hands over my face. One says, looking down at her new breasts, "My mom says we're all in stages of decay," and her voice sounds old when she says this. It sounds as though it's a hundred million miles away.

"If you don't breathe, you won't smell," another friend advises. "If you shut your eyes real tight, you can be in that other place in less than a minute. Don't even think or feel and boom! You're not even anywhere anymore."

Do-I-let. Allow. Toilet. Let. You must have let him. Why did you let him? You shouldn't have let him.

Toilet.

I look up places in books and imagine the ones with beautiful names; Senegal, The Fijis, Scituate, Mattawan, Indonesia, Fair Isle.

"Sometimes," another friend says, "it's like you can keep right on looking and see through mirrors and walls."

"Maybe mothers do it to their sons when they're nursing them and even probably, after."

Without saying who or when or how. Without even knowing that maybe we can question why, we talk in whispers, embracing ourselves with our own fear, afraid of what more might happen, what it might mean, afraid even to picture ourselves; little girls with our legs spread like those dirty women in the pages of our father's magazines, like those women walking back and forth along the same patch of sidewalk at night chewing gum loud, showing too much leg on too cold an evening, running up to cars, looking left and right before whispering "Hey mister" in those voices too full of sugar to be sweet. Little girls we are, little nasty girls who don't scream at the sight of those things coming toward us, who don't look up at those faces smiling down at us, who swallow, go blank as sky, don't cry out, just wait wait wait and it'll be over soon.

"Sometimes," one of my friends whispers, "my father gives me a dollar and then I go to the store and buy whatever I want."

"Once," another says, chewing on the rubber band keeping the edge of her braid together, "my mother's boyfriend gave me two subway tokens. I cashed them in and got a slice of pizza."

We can't say it. We don't know if this is what dirty boys write about on subway walls, the words that would make us anything else but a bunch of little girls. How can we dare, at eight, nine, ten, think of ever being anything other than little girls?

It ends this way. Without words or phrases or power. Without rage. It ends sorrowfully, full of hollow spaces, guilt, doubt. It ends swallowed, forgotten until someone wakes up one morning, half-whole, their arms wrapped around their knees, bound up in the weight of moving on, to the next place.

The next place.

And then I died again. But this was a different
death—hushed, billowing, vague.

Across the Street

JUNE 30, 1972

Marianna's mother's arms are flabby, Puerto Rican tan. When you are close, you can see the stretch marks near her shoulders and the tiny dimples at her elbows. Marianna is afraid she'll get shaky meat, the layer of flab that hangs down when her mother lifts her arm to wave.

I don't want shaky meat, Marianna says, pulling the tight skin beneath her biceps. *My mother even has shaky meat on her ass.*

You know what I don't want? Marianna asks, her eyes squinting into dashes. *I don't want anything that my mother got.*

Across the street a lady is screaming that her baby is drowning. Marianna and I run, our double dutch game forgotten for the moment.

A baby is drowning, my friend Marianna yells to her mother. But her mother doesn't leave her pillow in the window and Marianna runs on, without her. There are other mothers leaning on pillows in windows. Maybe because it is so hot. Maybe they are tired. The pillows are flat and gray.

The woman screams again and when we run into her apartment we find her baby asleep in the center of a stained mattress. The baby has her thumb in her mouth and Marianna, because she is older, leans over the baby and kisses it. The baby's name is Cassandra. Her cheeks are brown like the color of a Hershey bar. Her hair is brown too. When Cassandra grows up she will have a baby and learn to scream. Marianna and I, perched in windows the way our mothers are now, will watch her standing in the middle of the street, her legs spread, her head thrown back in fear, screaming, *Help me! My baby is drowning*, without running downstairs. We will watch the tears move slowly down Cassandra's cheeks without blinking. We won't remember this baby, so quiet with her thumb in her mouth, her eyelids fluttering, her lips curving into a dreamer's smile.

Outside, Cassandra's mother keeps screaming. Marianna says it is because when Cassandra was born, her mother lost her mind. *She still feels the pains*, Marianna says. *The pains*, Marianna says, *sometimes they don't go away*.

Dream of Shoes

Ten blocks from my house there is a shoe store run by a German man and his wife, Clare.

In the window there are saddle shoes, sneakers, loafers and lines of beige, black and brown orthopedics making heavy rows against the window's back wall. Separating the window from the shoes is a thin layer of yellow plastic, the kind used to line Easter baskets. The plastic gives the shoes an ancient look, as though they've been worn by a hundred people, then resoled, reheeled and shipped here for Clare and her non-English-speaking husband to sell.

"You want to buy?" Eyebrows raised, Clare peers out from the doorway to where I stand in front of her window, staring at the outdated, preworn shoes.

I shake my head.

"Then you *go!*" Her face twists into a grimace, as though she's smelled something unpleasant.

"I can stand here. Free country." I turn back to the shoes,

feeling Clare's eyes burning against the side of my neck, the top of my shoulder.

"*You* people," she shakes a yellowing, wrinkled finger at me. "You don't buy nothing here!"

I take a step back, away from the window, further away from Clare whose name we know because she begins most sentences as though she is making a phone call—*It's Clare. You want help, maybe?* The one time my mother herded us into the store, we left quickly because the inside smelled of old lemons and Clare barreled into us with *It's Clare. You want help, maybe?*, knocking my mother off guard with her swift-footed, stiff desperation. As we left, we could hear Clare behind us, *You people. You don't buy nothing here.* Though the four of us waited for one of my mother's snappy retorts, it didn't come. *I don't trust Germans*, my mother said quietly. *They give me the chills with those gray eyes.*

"I don't have money," I say apologetically. The desperation is still there, behind the anger, behind the sour lemons and yellow-shaded glass. I can see Clare—with her silent husband packing the old shoes into boxes and shipping them back to Germany, then for the last time, pulling the metal gates down on the empty gray store and taking their dream of shoes back to Germany.

"Yes, yes," Clare says softly. Her watery gray eyes take me in and there is no anger behind them now, just a sadness, a genuine sadness. "Nobody here with money," she sighs, waving her hand before retreating into the store.

What Happened Down There

JULY 15, 1972

Liza Maldonado, we call her Olga, I don't know why, takes me down to her basement where the darkness cloaks us in nine-year-old lust. Olga has one blue eye and one green one that my mother swears will keep her from ever acquiring a man of any sort of substance.

"What if she doesn't want to get a man," I ask.

My mother rolls her eyes, asks me if I've gone crazy. "Of course she'll want a man someday," she says. "Every woman does."

I feel my way to a straight-back chair and Olga straddles me then starts moving back and forth until the tight corduroys I am wearing begin to burn between my legs. Pulling Olga closer to me, I hear her breathing and try to kiss her but she turns her face away.

"No kissing," she whispers. "Kissing's bad."

"Then let me sit on *you*. I don't hardly feel anything."

"Wait till the feeling comes for me." She moves back and

forth across my lap a little while longer, faster. Reaching up, I can for a minute feel her breasts underneath her sweater. But she slaps my hand away.

"Only down *there*," she says, her words hard against my ear in the quiet.

I sit, waiting. When she tenses, then relaxes, we switch places, until the feeling comes for me.

"Get off now. You're heavy." I climb to the cement floor beside the chair. Olga strikes a match. In the second of light, we see an altar someone has just built—Mary and Joseph and Baby Jesus lined up across the room on a knee-high table. Olga cries out.

"We're going to die! God saw us!" The match flickers once and dies.

Olga goes to Our Lady of Mercy, the Catholic school three blocks from here. She says the nuns make her kneel in rice when she's bad and sometimes, if she thinks bad thoughts on her own, she spreads rice across the floor to kneel in. She says she always does this after we come up from the basement and maybe I should too.

"We have to get rice," I say.

Olga moans. "It's worse than that. It's like we cursed them. Somebody's going to die."

"That's a damn lie," I whisper. "God doesn't give a fuck. My brother . . ."

"It's not the same," Olga says. "We wanted it."

In the darkness, I hear her crying, softly at first, then louder and louder until I'm afraid the sound will carry through the ceiling into the living room where her mother is seated behind a cup of Café Bustelo, in front of "Days of Our Lives."

"We have to pray, Olga. Then nobody will die."

Olga sniffs. "We'll be punished bad though."

She lights another match, then finds a switch. Red light

fills the basement. Olga looks beautiful in it. But when I hold out my own hand, I look blue-black, like a creature.

Slowly, Olga moves toward the statues, crossing herself. When she is halfway to the altar, she turns.

"Come on!" She whispers. "Tell Jesus you're sorry!"

"Sorry . . . Jesus." I look at the statue of Mary but she is unforgiving.

Olga prays silently. "We have to wait for our punishment."

I am scared all of a sudden. Scared because if she let me, I would kiss her in front of a million Marys and Josephs and Jesuses. Scared that she won't let me again. Scared that I will always want this, no matter who's watching.

BabyJesus

JULY 16, 1972

From behind a *botanica* window, BabyJesus stares out, porcelain white, blank-eyed. Inside, candles line the shelves, white wish candles, green prayer candles, blue candles for the sick of heart and head, gold candles to make him love you, black candles to make her feel snakes crawling underneath her veins.

A Spanish woman behind the glass catches me staring, my nose pressed against the window, and beckons me inside.

"Todos," she whispers, lighting black incense and waving it in front of my face. *"Jesús mira todos."*

"No me *mira!"* From my friends, I have learned her language and she smiles. This dark little one must be from Panama, Santo Domingo, Costa Rica—islands far away from Europe, overrun with a darker-skinned people who, as if by accident, or a bad joke played on Castilians by God, speak the same language. I am shaking but I repeat myself. This time the English puzzles her. "Jesus isn't watching *me.*" The

thought of God no longer frightens me—the idea of this pale BabyJesus lurking behind the door of my bedroom, watching me while I bathe only makes me laugh now, make lewd gestures in the tub, underneath my covers.

But the woman is undaunted. Like many kids in the neighborhood, this dark one before her must too be bilingual.

"You don't be-lieve?" As though she is spitting because she hates the language I am forcing her to speak. As though English itself is a sin. She waves the incense closer to me. "To take away your bad." Then her eyes are rolling back inside her head and she is speaking a language I don't understand. Only when she moves closer to me do I realize that the incense smells of licorice and I am afraid. But she is holding me tight now, at the place where my neck meets my shoulders and I begin to cry, feeling the weight of my stomach as it presses down against my pelvis.

The woman smiles. There are gaps between her yellowing teeth. "Take Jesus into your heart," she warns.

Then I am breaking away from her and running, slamming out of the *botanica* door, running past the window filled with porcelain Marys and Josephs and sad looking ManJesuses with blood painted too brightly on their toes, the palms of their hands.

Behind me, BabyJesus is still staring blankly, still lying unswaddled in the dusty window display, yellowing with age, cracking underneath the weight of being holy.

The Places Where I Don't Belong

AUGUST 13, 1972

Months later there is a mall. Starting as someone's dream-scape, the plan was that it would tower over abandoned plots, adding an edge of newness to the surrounding decay.

"It makes everything look . . . sadder," my friend Marianna says. She is a month older than I am, Puerto Rican, sad as grace. We are walking past it slowly as if to examine the silver- and glass-elevatored building from every possible angle.

The tar streets surrounding the mall have been cobble-stoned and sparkle beneath our sandaled feet. Marianna and I walk carefully because it is August and boys, clumped to-gether in terrifying packs at every corner, are taking note; because our sandals are new, identical right down to the size—seven—even though I wear an eight and Marianna a seven-and-a-half.

A block in any direction away from the mall, melancholy gray tenements sag under the weight of their decay, held together by rusting pipes and masking-taped windows. From behind these windows, gray-faced children press their foreheads against the pane, looking wildly in every direction as though they have just missed someone important, as though maybe, if the heavy dark eyes look hard enough, they'll catch a glimpse of something beyond the black-gritted glass and yellow-brown tape.

"It's nothing," I say, disappointment surfacing. "Just glass and stores and . . . nothing." We had heard this would be a carnival, rides and dancers and shows. Rumors prevailing over our summer boredom. Maybe a circus we could join. Run away. Hide.

Marianna nods. "It's like when you dream you found a whole lot of money and then wake up and look under your pillow, right?"

Our fragile stabs at philosophy seem profound to us. We take our words, our thoughts, the way our thin bodies are learning to move as seriously as we take a math test, a punishment, our latest crush.

Marianna points to a child up in a window staring down at us. The child's hair is matted. She may be three or eight. There are lines in her face that seem as though they belong to someone else, someone older, able to contain sharp edges of sadness without crying out in pain. We perch ourselves in the center of a vacant lot on top of a pile of gravel, stick our arms out for balance and try to seem as though we're not watching the girl. But we are—sidelong—from the corners of our eyes. The girl's chin and cheeks are pointed.

"Maybe she lives by herself," Marianna says.

"Maybe she doesn't have anybody to feed her," I add.

"No." Marianna moves to the edge of the gravel, jumps off then climbs up to the top again.

"No." I follow her. "That can't be it."

Blocks behind us there is the mall, hung still with yellow, green, red and white GRAND OPENING flags. There are ice cream cones for kids accompanied by their parents. Someone has told us they're giving out toys if you buy something. I have a dime and two pennies in my pocket. Marianna has a nickel. Maybe later we'll buy a Hershey bar, split it in half then break off the perfect little rectangles one by one, to make it last, to make it seem like more.

The little girl is still looking at us and we are still making believe we are not watching her back. Then, skinny arms are struggling to push up her window. The arms seem disconnected, as though they belong to someone smaller who is kneeling down below her.

"Hey!" the girl yells, her voice scratchy and deep.

"Hey yourself," Marianna yells back.

"You better get outta there. You don't belong there! I'ma call somebody!"

"Call yourself!" I yell. The space separating us seems to grow wider. Our voices loud, struggle to fill it.

"I'ma tell somebody!" the girl yells again, then slams her window shut and continues to glare at us.

Marianna and I balance on the gravel stubbornly, our hands higher, like wings grazing the empty gray air.

"She thinks she's bad," Marianna says.

I nod, silently watching the girl full-out now. *Hey, little girl*, I want to say. *There are places you can go.*

"She probably don't even got a phone."

But I grab Marianna's hand and hold it hard until she cries out and calls me crazy. The little girl shakes her head slowly, stares at me, rolls her eyes.

I swallow. *Hey, little girl. You want to come with us to the mall?*

No More Nothing

AUGUST 31, 1972

Troy sends us letters from Vietnam. *We can take their scalps*, he writes. *We count them and the one who has the most, wins.* I ask my mother what do the winners get but her eyes fill. At night, she and my father whisper and hold each other and whisper and cry. Troy's absence pulls them into each other. Their desperation startles us. "It won't last," Angel says. But we listen, Tupperware cups pressed against the wall separating our room from theirs.

All the soldiers are so close here, Troy writes. *You wouldn't believe how close we've become.*

The summer before the war ends, a bullet catches Troy in the throat. Another one lands in the place where his thick brows meet between his eyes. *The war will make a man out of you*, my father had said to Troy. Someone had told my father about Troy kissing another man. *A man needs a good fight*, my father said.

We bury Troy in a closed black casket, a flag draped across the top. When I reach to touch my brother, someone grabs my arm, pulls it back. "Just the Afro pick," I scream. "It's still in his hair!" *No more letters from the front*, my sister says, tracing one of the stars. *No more nothing.* Angel presses a finger into my stomach. *This is where the pain goes*, she says and Carlos promises he will kill her and kick her down into the ground beside Troy if she says anything else ever again. But I rub the place where her finger was and swallow, feel sour saliva collect behind my teeth and swallow. Late at night, I sneak into my mother's closet, take a dress and heels from it and dance slowly around our room. *You would make a beautiful boy*, Troy had said. If I could feel him, pressed against me as we danced. If I could smell Mama's Tabu at the nape of his neck, see him stare longingly at the perfume's blue bottle, then maybe. . . .

In the blue-white light, I gaze at myself in the mirror, blue-black, kinky-haired, flat-chested. *Troy*, I whisper. *Troy Troy Troy Troy* until the words take on their own rhythm and Angel tells me to shut the fuck up and go to bed.

I don't sleep after Troy dies. Nobody sleeps after Troy dies. And the house becomes a haunted place, walls breathing in and out, hearts beating deliriously, skin on fire, *Hey girl, my skin's on fire.*

Go to sleep, Carlos says. *Make believe it never happened.*

We lower Troy into the ground without crying. Even my mother's eyes are dry. But when we climb back into the car, she moans. *My son. My son.* Then she collapses and my father rubs her eyes with spit to get her to open them.

Troy had an Afro. Omgauwa. Black Power. Destroy. White Boy. Left. Left. Left Right Left. My back is aching . . .

After he dies, our mother cuts my brothers' hair and Carlos's black naps mix in with Cory's brown curls. The hair lays on the kitchen floor for weeks until Angel wakes in the middle of the night, pulls a broom from behind the refrigerator and silently sweeps, sweeps, sweeps.

Crazies

After Troy dies, the other boys begin to come home crazy. Tar-black boys with broken bloodshot eyes. Yellow-skinned, nappy-headed hurting boys, their Afros cut down to impotent nubs, hands reaching out at the darkness, moving on their own, following the path of flailing arms, heaven-ward. Disconnected. Pretty caramel-colored boys staring off, distant and moaning. Chocolate boys with missing ears and arms running in circles around us, bewildered, begging, nod-ding off.

I see Miss So and So's son is home, someone would say and we run to see what parts of him came back alive, if any. We run to ask if he had known Troy over there and return home without answers.

If we had not been young, we would have died with our neighborhood, crumpled under the weight of its unfamiliar-ity, lost as the Crazies, anchored to nothing. The way their mamas cried out from behind cups of coffee, cried out into the blue light of the TV screen, their valuables clutched to them, hoping, hoping. Maybe these strangers in their house would leave again.

"Arriba! Abajo! Los Yanquis P'al carajo! Come up here," Marianna screams. She is perched on the base of a lamppost, her fist raised in the air, her wild black hair blowing. "Say it with me!"

"What are you saying?" I ask, climbing up on the lamppost beside her.

"Arriba!" Marianna screams. *"Abajo! Los Yanquis P'al carajo!"*

"Arriba!" I repeat, raising my own fist into the air. *"Abajo!"*

"Up! Down!" Marianna bellows. "Yankees go to hell!"

"I have to say it in Spanish, Marianna! My mother might hear."

Marianna nods. "It sounds better in Spanish anyway."

"Why we want the Yankees to go to hell?" I ask, glancing up and down the block for traces of siblings.

"The Mets is better," Marianna says, jumping down and hoisting her pants up.

"Who did your hair?"

"Angel. She straightened it. She burned the shit outta my ears too."

We head down the block, stopping to pick up Popsicle sticks.

"Ask your mother if you could spend the night. My mother's making *arroz con gandules.*"

"She's gonna say no." I pick up a Popsicle stick with a chunk of chocolate on the edge and fling it back into the street. "That's all she knows how to say since Troy died."

"Troy would've been crazy if he would've came home. Crazy like the other guys who was over there." Marianna fans her five Popsicle sticks like a deck of cards.

"No, he wouldn't," I say softly. "Nobody's crazy. Some of them just left a little part of themselves over there."

"That's bullshit. Everybody who went over there is all fucked up. Troy would've been too."

"Fuck you, Marianna," I say but the sentence is broken and half-hearted. Maybe Troy wouldn't have been fucked up.

"Fuck you back," Marianna says. When we turn the corner, she takes a cigarette from her pocket, leans against an abandoned building and lights it. The smoke circles above her head for a moment before dispersing. "I'ma learn to inhale one of these days," she says, handing me the cigarette.

We stand silently, feeling the sun hot against our faces. Tonight, maybe, if my mother says yes, I will spend the night at her house, have *arroz con gandules* for dinner, and rub against Marianna without words or sound until one of us swallows, goes still as death, then sleep. And in the sleep, I can forget about this zombie land our block has become, filled with Crazies.

"If Troy would've came back," I say, leaning beside her, squinting against the smoke. "It would have been different."

"That's a lie," Marianna says, almost in a whisper, like maybe she's rolling it around inside her head. She moves a step closer to me, and we stand like this, silent, smoking, two girls in T-shirts and shorts, our bare shoulders touching, waiting for the next thing.

Slipping Off

MARCH 1, 1973

"She's not supposed to fight back," Carlos says, peeking out from underneath his covers. "She's supposed to take it." In the pale light, he looks confused and small.

Cory listens to my parents fighting silently, his eyes wide. Years later, when he sends his girlfriend to the hospital with fractures to the skull, he will tell us that this is how a man teaches a woman to behave. And I will not remember where his lessons took place.

My father curses, cries out. Then I am farther beneath my covers, crying so that no one will hear—hard silent fearful tears. But Angel, lying in her bed beside mine, hears, touches me on the shoulder, says, *Shut Up, stupid. Nobody's dying in there.*

They fight in whispers but the blows fill up the silence. When my father is gone, Mama tells us there are things in this life she doesn't have to take. She says she believes in living. *I don't think that's asking for a whole lot.* She pulls us in close, kisses the tops of our foreheads and holds us as if living depended on it. *I don't ask for much*, she says.

Now, in their bedroom, my mother's whispers roll low from the back of her throat. "Damn you for taking this from me."

All of us are crying now, our stomachs tight, painful cramps against our fear. This fight is a new one. Maybe it's old. My father is drinking too much. My father has lost another job. The kids can't go hungry. They need clothes for school. There are bills to be paid. There are accusations. Lies. But behind all of this, there is something we haven't heard before. A finality. Heavy sighing. *Damn. Damn. Damn.*

My sister walks across the bedroom and tiptoes up to my big brother's top bunk. She whispers, *This is the grieving before the leaving*, because she is twelve now and has begun to talk in a language my little brother and I don't understand. My father cries out. This time my younger brother cries out with him. Then he is puking the plaster he has been peeling off the wall behind his bed and eating at night over the side of his bottom bunk, onto my sister's leg. Twice my mother has covered the wall then moved the bed away from it, but still he finds a way to peel the paint, stuff it into his mouth when no one is looking.

You're a dumb-ass, my sister whispers. But my brother is puking and crying and doesn't seem to hear.

Carlos is crying soft and low now. There is a rustle, then my father with his coat on, is walking through our room carrying a brown shopping bag spilling over with clothes.

Then my mother is in our room, snot dripping down onto her top lip, tears running down the sides of her mouth, cleaning up puke and crying, telling us to get to sleep, who do we think we are being awake at five in the morning. And the sun is coming through the window with all of this pink and gray mixed into it so I look over at my little brother who my mother is rocking back to sleep, holding what she can of him in her arms and letting the rest drape back across his mattress. I realize how pale and poisoned he is, how his skin looks green almost underneath the amber. My mother says it's from the plaster and the lead. I look at my sister who is back in bed staring at my mother like she wants to kill her or maybe just hurt her real bad. And I see my big brother, leaning down over his top bunk to watch my mother's face for some sort of sign but my mother just rocks and rocks even though my little brother has already fallen back to sleep with his mouth half-open and his tiny hands swinging. My mother blames everything wrong on the lead that's seeped into my little brother's blood and will probably end up in his brain too. When I ask now, she tells me this is why my baby brother is turning green. I point to the window, show her the colors setting the sky on fire. I ask her if my brother is green because my father has just slipped off, stare at Cory's hands, fisted and bent at his wrists like the bright hot wick of a birthday candle while I wait for her answer. But she is silent. My sister turns to me. *No, stupid-ass*, she whispers.

Then my mother is crying and telling my sister she'll beat her butt black-and-blue if she ever hears her call me a stupid-ass again.

Carlos asks my mother if daddy's coming back. When she doesn't answer he begins to yell, *Stupid-ass! Stupid-ass! Everybody's a stupid-ass!* until Angel, her eyes wide and wet, presses her fist into her mouth to keep from crying.

Cory wakes up moaning and my mother nuzzles her face against his neck.

I think, *Maybe this is happening to another family somewhere. Maybe all over the world fathers are stuffing their clothes into bags and slipping off.*

My mother puts Cory's crippled foot to her mouth and kisses it, softly at first then louder and louder until Cory is crying out and pushing her head away.

And all of this happening with the morning promising such a perfect, perfect day.

The First Time I Fall in Love

OCTOBER 30, 1972

The first time I fall in love, I yell up to Marianna's window and she yells down my name. This is her answer as though by calling out my name, she is telling me, I hear you. I see you. You are real. But standing on the curb, I pinch the skin on the back of my wrist between my thumb and forefinger and call her name again. "Marianna."

Marianna with her long hair and brown, brown eyes. Marianna with her new breasts and pretty toes painted bright red.

We sit in her backyard, across from each other, Marianna in the loveseat swing, me in a summer rocker.

"When we're old," I say, looking up at the sky, blue and clear as though the city isn't on the other side of this building *out front* as my mother says. "When we are old, we'll rock and rock and rock."

"Yes," Marianna says, wrapping her ankles around my own. "We'll be two old ladies together."

"Forever?"

"Maybe forever," Marianna says. And I still believe in forever, believe that we can remain two girls rocking here, with the world safe on the other side of us.

"Yeah," Marianna smiles, her eyes bright. "Maybe forever and ever."

And the world is perfect. So, so, perfect.

A million half-lives, some skirted but bare-chested, others naked. Some with dark arms reaching upward, others stooped into bending, still as glass. A million girls. Dark. Bellowing. Multiplying. Chaos. Hari-kari. War.

It's inevitable.

Sandra's beautiful, beautiful mother was found . . .

The Telephone Company
APRIL 15, 1973

Six months after my father leaves, my mother finds a job working until three A.M. at the telephone company. By 3:45 she is home. Through the thin walls, I hear her crying until blue-gold light fills the sky outside the bedroom I share with my sister and brothers. In the months to follow, a frown tiny and tight as a newborn's fist makes a permanent home between my mother's eyebrows.

One moment, please. I imagine the hint of Southern accent in my mother's voice going nasal over the wire. At the telephone company, my mother whispers to my sister and I when we are all three alone, the black women are forced to spread their legs once a month, to be checked for crab lice, gonorrhea, vaginal infections. The white women are free to hang their coats in the employee coatroom before moving to padded chairs at their stations, to drink coffee while waiting for their shifts to begin.

———

One moment, please. I dial O for operator when no one is home, imagine the face of the woman at the other end: Is she black or white? Has she been examined? Did they find anything *wrong?*

My mother tells us to keep our dresses down and our legs closed. From our relaxed position at the foot of her bed, my sister and I jerk our legs together, pull our dresses farther down across our knees. Angel takes our mother's lipstick and pretends to draw circles around her mouth.

"When I grow up," she says, "I'm going to have a roomful of makeup. Every single color everything. Be anybody I want."

"A black woman sees a hard time," my mother reminds us, applying heavy layers of light-brown face powder to the bags beneath her eyes.

"I'll paint my face white, then," Angel says.

"I don't want to grow up," I say. "I could stay little forever and wouldn't even care."

We watch our mother in the mirror, watch three perplexed faces peering back at us. We sit pressed into her on either side until she shakes us off, telling us growing up isn't anything to be afraid of; after all, look at her, she's living and doing okay. "But don't ever get so down that you have to take a job at the telephone company."

One moment, please. Do you stand up on a table when they search you? Does it make you have to pee? Why, when you're helping someone else, do you have to say please?

Playing Lessons

APRIL 21, 1973

"The man gets on top of the woman like this." Marianna demonstrates with a Barbie and Ken doll. "Then he puts his thing in her and she opens her legs like this." Marianna pulls Barbie's legs apart and moves Ken up and down between them. "It feels good for the man but it hurts the lady."

I watch her pull Barbie's bright pink blouse over the smooth plastic curves of her breasts. "He touches her here." Marianna touches Barbie's chest.

"Yuck!"

"You have to let him do it."

"No, I don't."

"If you don't, nobody's going to marry you."

We are sitting cross-legged, underneath the lining of last summer's swimming pool that we've constructed as a tent in the backyard. Outside the wind is blowing hard against the vinyl. Our tiny space fills with the warm air of our breath.

"If you close your eyes real tight, you can make believe you're someplace else when it's happening."

I move in closer to Marianna. She smells sickeningly of Love's Baby Soft, the perfume she stole from her older sister and sprinkled herself with too much of.

"I saw a man's thing last summer," Marianna confesses.

"You lie, you die!" I whisper wide-eyed.

"It was white and wrinkly."

"But black people have black things."

"I know *that*."

"And Puerto Ricans have Puerto Rican things."

"And Chinese people have Chinese ones."

We giggle. Marianna pulls Ken's pants down. "And Ken doesn't have anything!"

Now we are laughing louder, falling onto our backs and kicking our legs up against the fragile roof of our fort.

"I'm going to marry a man like Ken 'cause I don't ever want a thing in me!"

Marianna sits up and frowns.

"You have to," she says soberly.

"I don't have to!"

"If you don't, you'll grow a mustache 'cause when they do that to you something shoots inside you that keeps you a lady. If you don't have the stuff in you, you grow a mustache."

I sit up then and hug my knees. Marianna has dimples that cut deep into the side of her cheeks when she laughs, disappear when she doesn't.

We stare at each other without saying anything. My stomach feels queasy all of a sudden. *You'd make such a beautiful boy*, Troy had said. But he's dead now and Daddy's suits are long gone from the closet. When I take a bath and nobody's home, I take a knife from the kitchen drawer and keep it beside me. *I just want to . . .* Carlos says. But I tell him if he comes into the bathroom, I'll cut it off. *Don't fuck with me, Carlos!* I scream. There are places you can go when it happens to you but I've run out of beautiful names.

"Marianna . . ." I pull my knees in and stare at the blue plastic wall. Ken and Barbie are lying on their backs, far apart from one another.

"I don't want to be a man . . ."

"All you gotta do is once with a man and then it's all over. Plus, you won't die a virgin." Marianna smiles. "Then you come back to my house and we'll hang out."

I nod but don't say anything. Last month, my mother bought me a bra and showed me how to wear it. But I don't wear it and she says if I want to walk the neighborhood looking like a tramp, that's my business. If anything happens to me, she said, it'll be my own damn fault. I touch my chin. Maybe hair has already started to grow there.

"Let's do 'See, See, See,' " Marianna says, holding up her hands.

I clap mine against them, singing along with her:

> The sailor went to sea sea sea,
> To see what he could see see see,
> But all that he could see see see,
> Was the bottom of the deep blue sea sea sea.

Pantyhose

JULY 1, 1973

I want pantyhose like the ones my mother buys Angel.
The ones in the brown paper bag she carries into the bathroom. *I want pantyhose*, I scream through the thin sheath of wood keeping my sister at such a distance. But Angel emerges from the bathroom bare-legged, her face gray and drawn.

"How does it feel?" my mother asks, touching my sister's hair.

"Fine."

"I want pantyhose. Where are your pantyhose?"

My sister glares at me, calls me stupid then goes to lie down on the couch. When my mother leaves for work, my sister clutches her stomach and starts to cry, softly at first then louder and louder.

Leave me alone, she screams. *Everybody just leave me alone.*

My brothers and I watch her silently, afraid to get too close. Later, when my mother calls for my sister, they speak in whispers. Crouched in the corner of the living room behind a chair listening, I feel myself growing smaller and smaller. Maybe I will disappear.

"It's going to happen to you, too," Carlos warns me. "It happens to every lady. Then you have to watch your back."

At night I hear my sister in the bathroom, water trickling into the tub. When she climbs back into the high-riser beside mine, she seems to be surrounded by dampness. Lying beside her, I watch, half-asleep as her hands creep up to her stomach. Her sudden intake of breath, an indication that *this* growing is painful.

In the morning, her spotted gown hangs drying over the shower curtain. But there are no pantyhose, only toilet paper wadded in the wastebasket stained red with blood for days until my mother yells at her, *Don't be so nasty*, and I realize that getting your first pair of pantyhose is nasty. But it happens to every girl. Then every girl has to get up in the middle of the night to wash her gown. And watch her back.

Substitutions

Mrs. Hinde glares down at me when she thinks I am not looking. My mother doesn't believe Mrs. Hinde hates me for no reason.

"You must *talk* in class," my mother scolds, "or act out."

I deny these charges and believe my denial.

The school year moves slowly from fall to winter with me buckling beneath the impact of the Karo syrup smiles Mrs. Hinde reserves for the whiter-skinned Puerto Rican girls, buckling under her disdain, until the day she announces she will be leaving our fifth grade classroom for the rest of the year. We are sitting with our hands folded on our desks, Mrs. Hinde's rule, six rows, five across. I try to look upset and manage a major sigh but Mrs. Hinde shoots me a sidelong glare that lets me know she is unconvinced.

Mrs. Hinde is fat with pregnancy. She announces that Ms. Deluna will be replacing her. Then, as though on cue, the way I had been pushed on stage the week before to recite the three lines I had as Tom Sawyer's girlfriend, Becky ("Tom,

I'm cold. Tom, I'm scared. Look, Tom, it's Injun Joe!") a brown-haired white woman enters our classroom, looks straight at me, and smiles.

"I'm a feminist," Ms. Deluna says one morning. The classroom is hung in gray shadows from the overcast day outside. I am seated in the middle of the room, too far away from her, shivering in rain-soaked corduroys. "I don't believe men are better than women."

"Are women better than men?" I ask, calling out, the way Mrs. Hinde had never allowed.

Ms. Deluna looks over at me and cocks an eyebrow, a tiny smirk playing at the corner of her mouth—as though we're in on some secret together. The rest of the class is laughing at the ridiculousness of my question and the quivering voice in which it was asked. Ms. Deluna locks eyes with me, holds my gaze and winks. Her long hair is parted in the middle and hangs down in front of her shoulders. She doesn't wear a bra. I know this not because of the shape and bounce of her breasts under her sweater but because my mother told me all the feminists burned their bras and in twenty years they'll all be walking around with their breasts down to their ankles. I try not to stare at Ms. Deluna's breasts as I wait for her answer. She takes in the whole room before looking back at me. "Depends on who you're asking," she says.

My stomach dips down into my damp pants. When it resurfaces, Ms. Deluna has moved on to math.

That night I dream that Ms. Deluna and I are on a merry-go-round somewhere and Ms. Deluna has a firm hand on my back, keeping me on my horse. Merry-go-round music is playing in the background. When I lean over my horse to kiss Ms. Deluna, I catch a glance of Mrs. Hinde, standing off away from the merry-go-round with her arms folded. She frowns and taps her foot as she watches us. This doesn't stop me from kissing Ms. Deluna, hard; from reaching down and fingering her nipple beneath the sweater-blouse she is wearing. But I do all of this with my eyes open. And when my horse whirls back to where Mrs. Hinde is standing, I see that the woman there is my mother now, still frowning, still with folded arms.

Rituals

JULY 12, 1974

The ropes click and dance over themselves like something underwater—one up, one down, a school of fish following an uncertain leader.

Because it is summer I watch the ropes as though mesmerized, until my friends' chanting becomes the reverberating hum keeping time with the importance of the ropes' rhythm. A fragile ritual. A brittle perfection.

> All, all, all in together girls,
> How you like the weather girls?
> Fine, fine, super-fine.

I learn the ritual of jumping from my perch on a curb hard and hot with summer heat. At nine, ten and eleven, we are not allowed to participate in the game of double ropes, are offered a single one and listen with the hopes of being able to remember the songs to mimic later. And watch. In watching, we learn to respect—the quick-footed sureness of the teenagers.

> We hit them high, we hit them low,
> We hit them in the . . . well, you know!

We sit waiting, hoping. Maybe if we look like we know what we're doing from the sidelines, we'll be asked to join in—like the ten-year-olds my mother refers to as "fast" because of the nearly imperceptible sway of their hips, because of the swiftness with which they have learned to string together curse words, roll their eyes, move their shoulders in an argument, put their fingers in someone's face. We practice in front of the teenagers, try to show each other up from our line along the curb—cut our eyes, suck our teeth, whispering curses so that our parents don't hear. But mostly, we sit and wait and listen, listen, listen.

> Hey, Laura!
> Somebody's calling my name.
> Hey, Laura!
> Somebody's playing my game.
> Hey, Laura—he wants you on the telephone.
> If it ain't my honey tell him I ain't home!

"Collapse!" I scream, when I am finally invited to jump and the ropes fall in onto themselves, aborting my turn. This newness is so precariously allowed. One bad jumping routine, one flustered chant and it's back to the single rope and edge of the curb.

"It ain't no fuckin' collapse, you stepped on it you fuckin' liar!"

"Girl, I'll kick your ass, you call *me* a liar?"

"Whose ass you gonna kick?"

We stand, our hands pressed firmly against what will one day fatten into black girl hips, our eyes dark and frightened —sensing, sensing, what's to come.

> Ain't your mama pretty
> She got meatballs on her titties
> She got scrambled eggs between her legs
> Ain't your mama pretty?

The ropes, thin snakelike cords of white, the remains of someone's new clothesline, lay at the edge of the curb, abandoned.

"I'm gonna kick *your* ass!" said shakily, now neither of us is sure.

Someone yells, "Fight! Fight!" and soon there are dozens of people—kids, teenagers, and when I look up, one or two adults looking tickled by this—screaming around us, waiting, hoping.

Maybe there will be blood.

Other Lovers and Then, BJ

DECEMBER 1, 1974

"I'm young still," our mother says, gazing into her mirror. Her hair is dark but there are strands of gray running through it. Now she covers it with an Afro wig she keeps on a Styrofoam wig stand in her closet. Angel says, "Mama, that wig is for the revolution," and our mother sucks her teeth. Says, "It's about style. There's no revolution happening here."

But there is a revolution, even if it isn't sprayed with Wig-shine every Saturday night and fluffed out with an Afro pick. The revolution becomes the tight black dresses our mother wears and the tiny flirt that has appeared at the edges of her brightly painted lips. She wears the revolution like a flag and the dark black seams of it run a promise up the back of her legs.

"I'm young still," our mother says, kissing us good-bye every Saturday evening. "Young enough and pretty enough to get any man." And me and Angel believe her but Carlos says she's becoming a slut and if Daddy was here, he'd knock her sideways for showing her butt.

But my father is gone now, so our mother pulls lovers in and out of our apartment as though they are leashed. They are tall men and short, with bloodshot eyes and Afros, shaved heads and beards. Some bring toys when they come, bats and balls for my brothers, satin-skirted dolls with corn-silk hair for my sister and me. We treat these men with side-long indifference, accept their gifts like tolls allowing them entrance through our bedroom into our mother's.

The men leave noisily, in the sandy hours of morning without our acknowledgments, our preadolescent eyes sleepy, searching, apathetic.

On a cold night in December, my mother returns home stumbling and giggly with a man she introduces to us as BJ. We give him the once-over, searching his presence for gifts. Finding none, we murmur our disappointed hellos, then turn back to "Love American Style" until our mother yells for us to turn the television off because the sun will soon be up in the sky.

BJ stays, bringing with each visit a little more of himself until his razor and soap fill the dusting corners of our father's presence, his slippers peek out from our Daddy's side of the bed. When he thinks no one is looking, BJ sniffs the arms of the ragged man-tailored shirts left behind, smiles vainly into our father's mirror as he presses these shirts against himself.

BJ is smaller than my mother, stopping only at her shoulder, and this embarrasses us terribly. We tolerate his presence with measured distance, turn quickly back to the television when he enters and leaves, kiss our mother good-bye then stand awkwardly beside her, unsure of our good-byes around this stranger who smells each day more and more like our father.

BJ is formal, greeting Angel and me with two-handed handshakes, my brothers with single-handed ones. At night we hear our mother moaning softly.

"They're in love," Carlos whispers, leaning over the edge of his top bunk. Beneath him, we hear the hiss and crackle of plaster being pulled from the wall, then the sound of Cory chewing.

"BJ's gonna live here." Angel is lying on her stomach leaning on her elbows. "I don't even like him."

"What's not to like," I ask, moving closer to her. But she pushes me back to my own high-riser and gets up to pull our beds apart.

"You're the stupidest thing in the world," she whispers. "The absolutely, positively stupidest."

There are places you can go.

I raise up on my elbow and whisper, "It's just a game. BJ likes to play it."

Angel blinks, not looking at me but straight ahead, through the wall and into the room BJ and Mama share, on past it into the living room, out of the ceiling-to-floor living-room window, and even farther than that, her vision keeps moving, cutting through cement, and plaster, and people, and night.

Traveling

A train track, once the route of a freight train, now abandoned and in some places tarred over to make for an easy crossing of cars, separates the black neighborhood from the white one. We stand on our side of it, Cecilia, Sonia, Marianna and I. Cecilia is the toughest among us but we like to think we're all tough. Cecilia has a spray of white-headed pimples dotting her forehead, and teeth in dire need of braces. She is heavy, broad-shouldered, the only one of all of us not to get cut from The Braves, the all-boy softball team the fathers on our block put together. Sonia, Marianna and I don't like her but are too afraid to tell her so. On a hot day in July, two years from now, I will be the one to fight her, knocking a tooth from the side of her mouth, sending her, crying and bleeding, home. Her mother will storm down to my house to threaten my mother with a lawsuit, and the two of them, heavy women in housedresses, will have a fist-fight that the block will laugh about until I leave it, at eighteen. But for now, the four of us are standing on our side of the tracks, each of us daring the others to cross.

Cecilia is the first to see him. Then Sonia. When I finally understand what's got their attention, I see that the tall white boy they are pointing to is carrying a white bag with the big yellow McDonald's M on the front.

Cecilia is wearing flair-legged jeans that are too short for her and a tight T-shirt. Her tits are not really tits but fat masquerading. When she starts unlooping her belt from its hoops, the rest of us look on dumbly, scared of her next move.

"We're going to kick his ass!" Cecilia says, stepping over the tracks.

"What for?" I ask.

Cecilia glares at me. I try to glare back but my eyes can't go without blinking as long as hers.

The white boy is closer to us now. He is at least a head taller than I, the tallest of all of us.

"Charge!" Cecilia screams, swinging the belt over her head. Running ahead of her, I feel myself holding back, afraid of this, afraid of the weight and fear of him. The blood and bone of him. Charging into him, I try not to look at his face but can't help it. Tiny black hairs spew over his top lip. His eyes are bright gray—the color, my mother warned, of evil people. Behind me, I can feel someone struggling with the boy's legs. The boy is yelling but I don't hear it until his mouth contorts to form *"Nigger bitches! Goddamn nigger bitches!"* Then I am grabbing the belt from Cecilia and landing it hard across his face, arms, legs, chest. He rolls away for a moment but Marianna, Sonia and Cecilia are too fast, grabbing him before he can get to his feet. There is blood gushing out of his nose and from a split in his lip. Then he is crying and stumbling away from us and Sonia and Marianna and Cecilia are back on the other side of the train tracks, grinning, daring him to cross.

But I am still swinging the belt, screaming into the near-silent day, landing the leather hard against the street, the air, and the tarred-over tracks that still divide.

Trip to Cape Cod

FEBRUARY 10, 1976

We drive to a town at the edge of Cape Cod late in the winter. My mother drives the gray Chevy our father left behind with the slow uncertainty of someone unused to being behind the wheel.

"I'm going to show you the world," she announces proudly.

Carlos, beside her in the front seat, looks out of the window silently into the gray-blue dawn. White one-storeyed homes with somber windows move slowly past us.

In the back, I am seated between Angel and Cory. Each of them is staring out of a window, blank-faced.

My mother doesn't wear her wig anymore. And now, her soft, nappy hair curls down against the top of her neck. Where it stops, there is a small roll of brown flesh creasing into her back. I press my hand against my own neck and am relieved that there is only bone there, tiny sharp vertebrae jutting up into my skull.

In the rearview mirror, our eyes meet and uncertainly, my mother smiles. "You all need to see the world," she says to me as though she is asking for my okay. I nod although I know it is not the world she is driving three hundred miles to show us but the distance she can place between herself and BJ.

My mother cracks her window and a gust of February air forces itself in—air cold and thick as distance. I swallow, wondering if BJ's slippers are still peeking out from beneath my mother's bed.

"The Kennedys lived here," my mother announces. Then the car is moving through the town. "But we're going farther."

I look over my sister's shoulder. The houses loom larger for a while, set back away from the road and nearly hidden behind bare-branched trees. Then the cemented banks turn to sand and we are driving slowly, silently, as though we are strangers, as though our car is empty.

My little brother asks, *Where are we going?* and my mother answers, *To a place at the end of the world.* Then my little brother is crying and I am hugging him, whispering into his ear. I tell my mother, "He thinks we might drive right off."

In the rearview mirror, I see my mother's eyes empty out. "Tell him we won't." She sounds annoyed. Then to my brother she says, "Honey, I won't let you fall."

I swallow to keep from crying because I love her. I love her so, so much.

Carlos speaks for the first time in hours. "Are there only going to be white people at this place?" he asks as though he already knows the answer. Beside me, I feel my sister stiffen. We wait, lean into my mother, expectant.

Underneath the wheels of the car, sand crunches and

sprays back onto the banks. My mother looks again at the rearview mirror, checks my baby brother, sobbing softly in my arms.

To have this, four children leaning into her, adding to the weight of her with their own questions, their own expectancy, taking from the life of her their own new living; this is what she must have felt with five lives behind the wheel of one car—a gray hardtop Chevy—automatic, hard on gas but low maintenance otherwise and the insurance payment overdue so please don't let there be an accident.

I pull Cory closer to me and rub his head. Maybe he is sick. He's looking a little green. His prescription is in her purse but maybe there won't be enough money to fill it and feed everyone until it's time to go home. Angel has started her period but really there isn't enough money to give her her own room and now Carlos is asking the question everybody's been so afraid of since this morning when each of us brought what we wanted most out to the car: Carlos, his books of love songs, a stack so high she made him choose until he balked so she allowed them all and spread them evenly into the trunk so that it would close; Cory, a stuffed animal, a blue horse with one eye missing; and me—empty-handed. *I don't have anything I want to bring*, but Mama said, *Yes, you do. Bring those eyes*. Said, *Those hopeful eyes*, and smiled, telling me my eyes look straight into the soul of someone as though maybe I've lived before—staring everywhere, at everyone, now meeting hers every time she looks in the rearview mirror. *Child, where'd you get those eyes?* as though they are looking right into her brain reading every thought slipping through it. And Angel—her books, her books, so many of them Mama wondered where they'd fit and her journals and pens, so many pens that I asked, "Who could have that much writing to do?" and Mama said, "Don't worry about it." But I know she too wonders, what's Angel writing? Why won't she let anybody see?

Wondering what she is saying about you and BJ who you walked in on early one evening and caught straddling her, your oldest girl, your pride, him straddling her like she was you or a common whore or a woman but no, she was your child and him taking her like that right in your bed and you not being able to help but meet her eyes and see all the fear there, all the hate for you because this was the bad dream that came in the night and you weren't there to hold her, tell her everything would be all right. This was the bogeyman you had sworn to protect her from, the darkness she had been afraid of as a child—those journals. What is she saying about you there? Why doesn't she look at you anymore? Why can't she remember how you nearly killed that man until the cops came and rescued him, bloody and small, screaming apologies into the space that had become so void of air you had to rescue us from it?

To here—where is here? And now Carlos, sitting beside you silent and empty as a day before snow, asking the question that you had not thought of because all you really wanted was to get so far away from that vision, BJ and Angel.

Are there only going to be white people at this place?

And now your answer coming soft and slow, *It doesn't matter,* resigned because it really doesn't. Just so long as there are people, people who couldn't possibly know, people who won't acknowledge what goes on in some homes while the mother's out working, trying to feed four kids and the kids growing, growing, bleeding her dry with their growing, learning to hate her in their growing and her not knowing where she went wrong. How could she have gone wrong? How does she do this right and still live? These children, these children that scream *I didn't ask you to bring me into this world*, and they didn't so why did you?

And now the baby crying, afraid, afraid you're taking us to the edge of the world so that you can drop us, one by one, off.

How could you have known that this was motherhood? How could you have known when Troy was poking the first moments of his life out from between your legs that this was the beginning of a loss of control? That while inside you, you could protect us, feed us, love us without distance, touch us with only skin separating you and even that skin was not as thick as the air that separates you now. How could you have known that this was motherhood? Your own parents dead before you were grown, who could have warned you?

It really doesn't matter, you say out loud to yourself. Because it doesn't, not now, not anymore anyway.

Then Angel's vacant eyes catch a glimpse of the ocean, light up for the quickest second and in the rearview mirror, I see a smile curl up and you wink at me. And I wink back. Maybe, maybe you've done the right thing.

Coney Island at Easter

EASTER SUNDAY, 1976

M y mother doesn't see me watching her count the dollars and quarters she saves in a jar then pours into her purse on Easter Sunday. She tells us that we can have one ride and one snack at Coney Island before she hustles us onto the F train and stands guard as the doors close, as though one of us may decide to jump out at the last minute and run.

When the train emerges from its tunnel, Cory screams, *Outside! Outside!*, and pulls himself up on his knees to get a better look at the tops of buildings and tiny cars passing below.

I sit with my hands in my lap acting as though I don't care until Angel says, *You know you want to look, too*, and I hate her, because she's right.

A year has passed since my mother's ex-boyfriend, BJ, took Angel up on The Cyclone. When they came off the roller coaster we all crowded around her. She had been the bravest but my brothers and I, even though we were too afraid of the ride, still wanted to know what it was like.

Scary, my sister said. *It was scary*. But she walked far away from BJ after that and I knew it wasn't the ride that had been scary but what happened up there in the middle car on the rickety tracks. Maybe before the roller coaster dropped down and took everybody's air with it. Maybe after.

Which ride, my mother asks now as we gather around her, our mouths and hands sticky with cotton candy. *No roller coasters*, my mother says. Angel looks away. She knows she has ruined it, everything for everybody, forever.

Liberty

JULY 4, 1976

There are fireworks shooting out from behind the Statue of Liberty. The crowd *oohs* and *aahs* and I stand, sardined among a hundred thousand other New Yorkers crushed into Battery Park for this glorious bicentennial Fourth of July. At least that's what the newspapers are calling it.

Two blonde girls walk past me dressed as pilgrims. In a picture from a textbook I see the outfit I would have worn then—tattered burlap sacks with holes cut out for arms. I stick my tongue out at the pilgrim closest to me. Give her the finger. Her blue eyes open wide then look as though they're about to tear. I want to pinch her but too quickly she is pushed ahead in the crowd by more pilgrims.

Liberty's face does not change and I wonder if she too is thinking that this is all bullshit.

"Hold your sister's hand," my mother commands. "That's all I need is to lose one of you."

Angel's palm is sweaty and reluctant.

I get lost anyway, swept apart from my family when a firecracker is thrown into the crowd. Someone steps on my toe, shoves me into a woman holding her baby tight to her chest. Then I am stranded in Battery Park surrounded by people I've never seen before. My stomach surges, dips down into my back then surfaces somewhere in my throat.

"Mama . . . ?"

No one answers.

Orange and red and blue light pops and crackles out of Liberty's back. On my right wrist a blister, still tender from a soap pad tied on the end of a string that I lit then swung around in the air to create an eerie firelight the night before, oozes blister liquid.

"Mama . . . ?"

A heavy black woman approaches me, puzzles for a moment, then hurries past.

"I'm lost, somebody." The words aren't louder than a whisper but it seems everyone around me hears and no one responds.

An old man walks up to me as though he is about to say something, as if I am the little girl he has been searching this crowd for; his lost granddaughter, his niece, a child of a family friend allowed to accompany him because he is so trusted, so caring. But when he is closer, I see that his thing is dangling outside of his fly, pink and wrinkled with impotence and age.

"Little girl . . ."

"I'm lost . . . mister."

He looks nervous for a moment. Then his hand is moving back and forth along the length of his thing. I watch it, mesmerized. After a few moments, he too moves on.

The tiny space between my legs goes numb. I press them together. Maybe I have to pee.

People move quickly, brushing against me on all sides.

In the heat of July, sweat drips away from the new hairs under my arms.

Somewhere, in the back of my head, I know to call a cop, to give my address, my phone number. Policemen move back and forth through the crowd, keeping chaotic order.

Watching them, I realize that this is a good loss. There is direction to it, or at least a chance of direction beneath the doubt. This is what it must feel like to be grown. This is what it must be like to be free.

Frozen

Angel is the only one who doesn't come back from Cape Cod whole. She comes back naked, evil, raw. *I hate this house*, she screams. *Hate these little rooms. Hate you.* And our mother winces but doesn't say anything. She has sprayed each corner with Lysol, has lit candles and incense and sage. But the essence of BJ still prowls and Angel grows distant from the rest of us, enraged and silent.

When she falls in love, she hides behind her journals, sings stupid love songs at the top of her lungs.

Now, naked, as though she is frozen, my sister stands in front of our mirror.

It's like Forty Going North then it's over. But to be that close to someone—so close that you open your mouth and taste their breath, that's what love is. She whispers this to me when no one is home. When no one is home, she strips, checks for hickies and other signs that may tattle to the world.

I tell her I know what it feels like. When she looks at me, her eyebrows raised, I am silent.

Slowly, my sister moves her hands down her waist to the new round of her behind. Her eyes are glazed, dark and flat as the leather jacket she pulls her naked body into now, pulls close to herself.

Where are you? I want to scream standing in the doorway of our room, invisible.

My sister has a new lover, her first, a boy with brown hair curling over the pimples dotting his forehead. *White trash boy!* my mother screams when my sister tiptoes back into our house just as dawn is opening the sky to day. Then my mother is over her, hands flying, swearing she'll show my sister who has control.

Control. *Angel can't be controlled,* my mother cries to her friends. *I don't know what's wrong with that one, I can't control her.* Her friends nod their heads wearily. Weary yeses, weary side to sides.

The leather jacket is ragged and patched with duct tape under the arms. *His* jacket, a loan to keep her warm as she snuck back out into the night, to protect her from my mother's raging, to let others know she belongs to him now, that he has control.

As though dreaming, my sister walks across the room, lies down on the bed, parts her legs.

Where is this?

I watch her touch herself, moving her hand back and forth faster and faster until it blurs, or maybe I am crying. She sighs, brings her fingers to her nose and smiles. She is alone with herself, unaware that there are four walls, a ceiling above her, a sister behind her. Unaware and frozen in her moment of new love like nothing she's ever felt before shooting hot from the presence of the white trash boy who moves toward her like a heater or sun or fire, until she can't decipher his touch from her own.

If you do it with someone you don't love, it ruins you, my sister warns. *It'll never feel good with anybody then. BJ tried to ruin me. You have to be stronger.*

I stand watching her, letting tears trickle down into the sides of my mouth. Rain slams against our bedroom window, silvers against the sill. I look past Angel, into the slate gray morning, afraid of my sister. Afraid to follow her into this.

Another layer is added by the process of taking away . . .

Autobiography of a Family Photo

MARCH 15, 1978

Angel wants to wear black stockings but my mother says no, matter of fact as if it is that easy, and continues to apply eyeliner, her lips turned downward as though this helps the horizontal motion.

"Not with a white dress," she says. "You'll look like a whore."

The stockings hang from my sister's right hand like the murky slaughtered estuaries of horror movies. In her other hand, she is fingering a garter belt that my mother has given her and shown her how to manipulate.

"Wonder where I learned it," my sister mumbles, out of earshot of my mother.

I am dressed in my favorite outfit—a brown suede miniskirt with strips of a darker brown leather running horizontally from waist to hem, a white sweater, black tights and patent leather shoes. Cornrows travel down the back of my head and dangle entwined in colored rubber bands at my shoulders.

"Your mama's girl outfit," Angel sneers, kicking me as she passes.

My mother doesn't see this and I am trying to control my tattling.

I stand beside my mother, watch her put on makeup in the tarnished mirror that hangs above a dresser at the foot of her bed. "How can we take a picture without Daddy?" I ask, even though it has been years since our father slipped off.

"We just can."

"But how? Then it's not even a family."

"People do it," my mother says. "People survive. We've survived."

"It's not the same. It's not a family. It's like our family isn't real."

In the photo, my sister is wearing black stockings. My brothers are dressed in jackets and ties. They are standing behind us, in front of my mother. No one is smiling. In the photo, I am looking up at my sister, my face turned away from the camera so that one side is shadowed in darkness. It is as though the picture is fading even as the camera flashes, its edges curling up like paper on fire.

My sister grows up to marry a Jehovah's Witness and writes me often. *There will come an end to this system of things*, her letters warn. *God has had enough.*

In the picture it is as though I already know this, as though the words are there already, festering inside my sister's brain, waiting to explode. My baby brother looks frightened. Maybe there are things he knows too—that one day he will discover heroin and he too will begin to fade. And my older brother—that he will have daughters who grow up afraid of his presence.

When I visit my mother years later, the picture is framed

still, on the mantelpiece in her living room, yellowing, shrinking with age, my baby brother's gold skin turning green. *Are you ever going to get rid of that dumb picture?* I ask.

She shakes her gray head slowly, mouths, *Never*, because she has lost the ability to speak out loud, and the doctors can't tell us why. So we lean in close to her, visit rather than call, watch her face in the hopes of understanding her. *One moment, please.* And every time her mouth circles a word, I hear her long-ago voice, asking strangers to hold on.

Never, she mouths again as if she cannot see the picture, as if she doesn't remember why none of us are smiling, why there is still a faint dark ring and puffiness circling my sister's eye.

Long after she is old and silent, my mother holds on, learns to write quickly, to type into a TTY. She writes, *Keep the things* to me and sends this letter with a Polaroid of Angel, Troy, Carlos, Cory and me bundled up at Coney Island. Troy is standing back, away from us, but in the photo he is reaching for my hand. *Girl, you would make a beautiful boy.* He is smiling at me, and winking. I keep this and other things. I grow up hollow, misdirected, fractured, move from place to place, job to job. Last winter I drove back to Cape Cod, parked at the beach and walked fully clothed into the water. Maybe I wanted to keep going. Behind me, a woman called out. *Hey, it's too cold*, she yelled. But I kept walking until the water was up to my shoulders. Then I walked a little farther, stood shivering while waves broke against my face.

Hey, the woman called. *It's too cold. You don't belong there.*

Later

I am kissing Daniel Vicente inside my vestibule when the lights go out. "The fuse," I say, pushing him away from me. "My mother will come down to change the fuse." But Daniel pulls me close to him again, and sucks my lips into his own. He is so beautiful he is almost white, and that is so beautiful because I am older and there is only white that's so beautiful anymore. The day before my mother tells me, *The more coffee you drink, the blacker you get*, and I push my coffee cup away from me, afraid that I will get darker than I already am, afraid the kids at school will stop picking on Valroy—blackie, blackie Valroy, hurry on down to Hardee's, where the Valroys are charcoal broiled Valroy—and turn on me. I push my coffee away from me, go outside where light-bright Daniel Vicente is spinning a top and touch his arm. *You want to make it with me later, Daniel?* Later the other boys will call me a 'ho and say I'm easy as pie, kiss the boys and make them cry. But Daniel nods, says, "I gotta go home tonight but how about tomorrow in your hallway," and I say okay. I know Claude told him I kiss good and if he says he loves me I'll let him touch my breasts but not inside my blouse even if he says it. I know Evan told him he can probably get a little bit from me if my mother isn't around but I don't care. I really don't. If he loves me that's okay too. It's nice to be loved even if deep inside I know it's not for real.

But it isn't a fuse. It's a blackout and people are running up and down the street when we come out of the vestibule, our lips swollen and red, my breasts sore where Daniel pinched them too hard trying to feel underneath my T-shirt and bra. Shadows run up and down the block screaming, "Blackout! Blackout! Everywhere is dark!"

Then my friend Marianna is running past. "I'm going to Broadway. Everybody's going to Broadway 'cause all the stores, the alarms don't work."

My mother brings a pillow to the window and watches the people. "I don't want none of you leaving the gate," she says to us. Angel and Carlos beg but my mother just shakes her head watching the people run up and down the block.

I see Marianna again and make her promise to bring me something back. Later, she returns with boxes from Shoe Town. *I couldn't find your size*, she says.

"You two go find some soda and a bag of ice," my mother says to my big sister and brother, throwing down a sock with money in it. "Come right back."

But they don't come right back. They come back later with shoes and shirts from Buy Rite. My mother cries and screams when she sees the stuff but Angel keeps saying over and over, "But we got it for free. The store was wide open." My mother takes the stuff to the front gate, pours Mazola oil over it and lights a match. When the fire goes up, there is so much light that for a moment, people stop and watch.

"No child of mine . . ." my mother keeps saying. "Never, a child of mine . . ."

But Angel is hiding a shirt behind her back. Later, she will put it on.

The Feeling

SEPTEMBER 1, 1977

Sometimes I touch myself. Knowing this is something I can't tell anyone, I write it down in a diary that has a tiny silver lock on it. The diary is pink with the face of a white girl with black hair parted in the center and hanging down past her shoulders. *It feels good*, I write. *The way it used to feel when Carlos touched me, only better*, and the girl on the cover is smiling like she understands everything. Like she had a big brother once too.

My legs close up around my hand like they have their own mind and my fingers start moving faster and faster. Then there's a feeling like my stomach is going to explode. Then for a split, split second, everything in the world is perfect.

Marianna comes over one Sunday at the beginning of fall to ask if I want to go shopping for school clothes.

I have a thing to show you, I say.

In the bathroom, I take off my shorts and panties and lie on my back under the water faucet.

The water feels good like this, I say, opening my legs to

let the water wash against me. *You can get the feeling.* Marianna knows what the feeling is. A long time ago, we used to rub against each other when we slept over. Then we got the feeling. But Marianna has a boyfriend now, a tall Puerto Rican guy named Jesús. She says his thing is big but she has never really seen it. She says she wants to wait until she's married.

What if you don't like the way it looks. What if it feels bad?

"I'll have to take a chance," Marianna says. "With love, sometimes you have to take chances."

"It washes you out, too," I say now. I can hardly say anything because the feeling is coming and I think about nuns, pulling their habits up to show me underneath.

Marianna watches me for a moment before turning away.

"You should get a boyfriend," she says and quickly as it comes the feeling fades. Snaps off like a light, like something there never was.

One More

Marianna's mother checks all the girls' panties once a month and if there isn't a little blood in them, she has a fit. Marianna's oldest sister Frances cuts herself and wipes her bleeding finger against the seat of her panties for months and months until her stomach is so big everybody, even her mother, has to admit it's time to make room for one more. Then everybody's stomach on the block seems to be growing and my mother calls my sister and I into her room for a little talk.

If you ever, she says and my sister and I promise we won't.

But one night I hear my mother talking to her friend. *I know it will be her if anybody*, she says about me. I press my nails into my palms until they bleed. *It won't be me*, I want to scream. *Not now. Not ever.*

Frances's baby is born with six fingers on each hand. Her mother says it's a sign from God that the baby is special but the hospital cuts the extra fingers off anyway and the baby grows up with tiny nubs where only the smooth edge of hand should be.

Frances puts the baby in front of "Josie and the Pussycats" every Saturday morning and together, they watch all the cartoons from eight o'clock until three in the afternoon. Sometimes, Frances puts her breast in the baby's mouth when she cries and this shuts her up but Frances has breasts that are all the way down to her stomach.

"I'm going to have a band," Frances says, but Marianna and I laugh.

"Not with those titties," Marianna says. "You have to have high ones to be in a band."

Frances thinks her breasts will get high again but her mother says they won't. She says once they're down, they're down to stay. She says some ladies get an operation to make them high again but Frances doesn't even have a pot to piss in 'cause if she did, her mother says, she would buy the baby formula and maybe have a little left over to buy herself some Jolly Ranchers, the apple ones that she likes so much even though they turn her tongue green.

"You gonna have a baby?" Marianna asks me.

"No. I don't want that thing to happen to my titties."

"It happens anyway," Marianna says. "When you get old, you can wear a bra all day long, but at night when you take it off, boom, they fall down to the floor. And every morning you have to pick them up again. If you have a baby, they just fall faster. Everything in your life falls faster when you have a baby. Everything."

We stare at Frances in front of the television, her little baby tucked underneath her sagging breasts, her face old and pinched as though she is forty instead of seventeen and I grab my tiny breasts in my hands and hold them, hold them.

Like Nothing
APRIL 24, 1978

My sister runs away and joins a commune. She sends us a picture of herself with a flower in her hair and my mother says, *What a pretty flower*, then she covers her face with her hand, crying softly into it as though she can disappear behind it. I stare at her brown, brown fingers then look at my own hands, the one that holds the picture of my sister and the empty one. My hands are like my mother's. They are dark and the fingers are long. Behind the nails there is a beige color, like my little brother's skin.

"She's nineteen," my mother says. "She can do what she wants." *Everybody, all of you*, she starts yelling, *go do what the fuck you want*, and we scatter—everybody except Carlos who stays behind to hold my mother up. He is twenty now. He could have done what he wanted a long time ago but he didn't. Maybe he is afraid.

Are you afraid? I ask Cory when we are outside. Up and down the block there are children, so many children, the children of my friends who are my age and for a moment I want a baby of my own but know I shouldn't because I am only fifteen. But I want one so badly, some little somebody to love the way all the girls love their babies, cuddling them and dressing them up in beautiful little outfits. I want some little somebody to call my own, to take from here with me into another place, far away.

"Everybody's scared of something," Cory says. He tells people he is Puerto Rican when they ask why he is lighter than the rest of us and when they ask how, he shrugs and says, *Just because*, and it makes me think he is afraid to be black the way the Puerto Ricans say they're Italian sometimes because they think maybe that is better. But there is nothing I can say I am.

My new boyfriend is Gregory and he says he loves me, that maybe one day we'll marry. All the other girls are jealous. Behind my back they say, "How did someone so black get somebody so fine," and I hold on to Gregory because I'm afraid he'll leave. My friend Marianna says have his baby then he'll have to stay. But she has a baby now and no man. When she comes outside to push the baby up and down the block, she wears tight clothes and my mother says, *That's how she got the first one*. Everybody looks at me, wondering how I escaped. I make Gregory pull it out before anything happens. But Marianna says she tried that and a little leaked out before. Once, I held Gregory's butt and begged, *Give me a baby, please! Just one little baby*. But he is stronger and says he isn't ready. Marianna says this is a sign that he doesn't really love me.

Maybe your guy's playing you dirty or something, Marianna says.

"What are you scared of?" Cory asks. He straddles the cement divide that separates our house from the next and looks out over the block. It is too cold for April. A picture of my sister flashes in my head. Is she warm enough wherever she is? Does she think she found God there?

"I'm not scared of anything," I say.

Then Marianna walks past with her baby.

"You sure grew up to be fine," she says to my brother. "Stop by sometime or something," she says, taking a drag from her cigarette and blowing it out of the side of her mouth. "I'll cook you something nice."

My brother nods and I move closer to him.

"What's it look like from up there?" I ask, shoving my hands into the pockets of my jeans. *Why don't you wear a dress sometimes*, Greg asks and I tell him I hate dresses, that I like the way they look on other girls but not me. He looks at me sideways when I say this but is silent. Marianna's butt jiggles down the block. She looks back once, winks at Cory and continues. A week ago I asked her if she remembered the games we used to play and she said, *Not really. Just a little bit*. Like how I always wanted to kiss her. But she wouldn't look at me when she answered.

Anyway, we're too old for that stuff, huh? I said.

Yeah, Marianna. That stuff's for little kids.

"Huh, Cory? What's it look like?" As though I haven't straddled that divide a million times.

My brother shrugs. "Like nothing."

The Beautiful Ones

AUGUST 1, 1979

Brenda and Maraya from down the block have a fistfight over Cory and he watches, laughing at them. When they are pulled apart, bloody and small-looking, Cory walks away as though he's never seen them before.

"You shouldn't . . ." I say to him.

But he just says *fuck you* and glares at me. A long time ago he picked up a cigarette and began smoking. Now he is encased by smoke, and the smell of it, hard and stale, creeps from his pores. "You don't know anything," he says. "That's why Greg left your ass."

Cory and I stand like this for a long time until he lights a cigarette, coughs once, and turns away, taking quick strides down the block, until his feet seem as though they will lift off, like a helicopter, and fly.

"I should have killed her," Brenda says, a few days later. "Ugly yellow bitch." She tosses a head full of fake hair from her eyes and grins.

"Did you give Cory some?" I ask, raising an eyebrow and

shoving both hands in my pockets. *You look like a dyke*, my mother says when she sees me do this but I shove them in there anyway and walk around the neighborhood not caring that the seat of my pants is dirty from sitting on the curb without putting any newspaper down, even though my friends have started caring about the way they look. Not caring that everyone thinks I walk like my father. As if anyone can remember. As if anyone can remember anything.

"A little bit," Brenda says, looking off. She doesn't have any babies so I assume she knows what to do. People say there is something wrong with her, that she is a little off, that she laughs too easily, too loud, too long. "I love him," Brenda says.

Across the street, Cory is sitting with a girl who has just moved into the neighborhood, his arm around her pale shoulder. Brenda makes believe she doesn't see this. The girl has hazel eyes that make the small girls on the block flock around her. *She's so beautiful*, the tiny girls breathe. *She's like a movie star.*

My brother's new girlfriend looks over at us.

When they kiss, Brenda's eyes fill up.

"Let's go walk," I say. "There's really nothing happening around here."

We walk for a long time without saying anything.

"What are you gonna do, Brenda?" I ask, as though I have asked this a hundred times before. I ask this like a grown-up, try to sound as though I really care.

"I'll kick that new bitch's ass too," Brenda says. "I'm not afraid to fight. You gonna try to get your man back?" She looks at me from beneath her eyelids. There is too much fear behind her gaze, too much hopelessness, even though her lips are poking out. Even though she's trying to appear brave.

"Fuck him."

There is an aloneness taking hold now, slowly, like something thick and hot filling me up, piecing me together. I am told I am too skinny, too dark, too angry. My mother shakes her head, says she wants to find the beginning of my evilness so she can pull it up by its roots. But the roots are planted too deep, have been growing for too long. And now, their massive limbs are surrounding this aloneness. . . .

Brenda and I walk and walk and walk, circling the block a few times before veering off, away from it, toward another neighborhood. Brenda folds her arms across her chest and follows a step behind me, uncertainly. *Where are we going?* she asks when the neighborhood becomes white, unfamiliar. People stare at us, glare, cross to the other side of the street. Maybe someone will shout, *Hey! You don't belong here*, so I can barrel into them, the full force of these raging years.

I start walking faster and Brenda struggles to keep up.

The sun moves behind us, feeling warm and soft against my back. My hair is in a thousand tiny beaded braids that brush against my shoulders. Now I grab it up in my fists and scream till my throat is on fire. Brenda laughs. Maybe she thinks I'm crazy. Maybe I am. Then I grin, throw my head back and laugh out loud. Brenda looks puzzled for a moment then she's grinning too. Standing there, watching me. *Come on*, I say. But she shakes her head *no* and waves good-bye. When I start walking again, it's as if I'm walking to save my life, as if I'm walking to get out of some bad story where I'm the pitiful one. As if I'm walking right off of somebody's dumb, otherwise blank page.

ABOUT THE TYPE

The typeface used in this book is a version of Sabon, originally designed in the 1960s by Jan Tschichold (1902–1974) at the behest of a consortium of manufacturers of metal type. As one who began as an outspoken design revolutionary—calling for the elimination of serifs, scorning revivals of historic typefaces—Tschichold seemed an odd choice, but he met the challenge brilliantly: The typeface was to be based on the fonts of the sixteenth-century French typefounder Claude Garamond but five percent narrower; it had to be identical for three different processes, working around the quirks of each, such as linotype's inability to "kern" (allow one character into the space of another, the way the top of a lowercase *f* overhangs other letters). Aside from Sabon, named for a sixteenth-century French punchcutter to avoid problems of attribution to Garamond, Tschichold is best remembered as the designer of the Penguin paperbacks of the late 1940s.